W9-AHF-454

IS TAFFY FOR REAL?

Taffy wants to help me? Jana thought in disbelief. It was impossible. They had *always* been enemies.

"What kind of plan?" Jana asked. She braced herself to hear some obviously devious ideas.

"I want you to remember that I won't do this if you say not to." Taffy seemed to be considering how to tell her. "I think if *I* asked Randy to be *my* partner on the Family Living project, Laura couldn't ask him, and then she couldn't steal him away from you. I'd only do it because I want us to be friends. . . ."

Bantam Skylark Books by Betsy Haynes
Ask your bookseller for the books you have missed

THE AGAINST TAFFY SINCLAIR CLUB
TAFFY SINCLAIR STRIKES AGAIN
TAFFY SINCLAIR, QUEEN OF THE SOAPS
TAFFY SINCLAIR AND THE ROMANCE MACHINE
  DISASTER
BLACKMAILED BY TAFFY SINCLAIR
TAFFY SINCLAIR, BABY ASHLEY, AND ME
TAFFY SINCLAIR AND THE MELANIE
  MAKE-OVER
TAFFY SINCLAIR AND THE SECRET ADMIRER
  EPIDEMIC
THE TRUTH ABOUT TAFFY SINCLAIR
THE GREAT MOM SWAP
THE GREAT BOYFRIEND TRAP

Books in The Fabulous Five Series

  #1 SEVENTH-GRADE RUMORS
  #2 THE TROUBLE WITH FLIRTING
  #3 THE POPULARITY TRAP
  #4 HER HONOR, KATIE SHANNON
  #5 THE BRAGGING WAR
  #6 THE PARENT GAME

THE FABULOUS FIVE

The Parent Game

Betsy Haynes

BANTAM BOOKS
NEW YORK • TORONTO • LONDON • SYDNEY • AUCKLAND

RL 5, 009-012

THE PARENT GAME

A Bantam Skylark Book / March 1989

*Skylark Books is a registered trademark of Bantam Books, a division of
Bantam Doubleday Dell Publishing Group, Inc.
Registered in U.S. Patent and Trademark Office and elsewhere.*

*All rights reserved.
Copyright © 1989 by Betsy Haynes and James Haynes.
Cover art copyright © 1989 by Ralph Amatrudi.
No part of this book may be reproduced or transmitted in any form or by
any means, electronic or mechanical, including photocopying, recording, or
by any information storage and retrieval system, without permission in
writing from the publisher.
For information address: Bantam Books.*

ISBN 0-553-15670-5

Published simultaneously in the United States and Canada

---

*Bantam Books are published by Bantam Books, a division of Bantam Double-
day Dell Publishing Group, Inc. Its trademark, consisting of the words
"Bantam Books" and the portrayal of a rooster, is Registered in U.S. Patent
and Trademark Office and in other countries. Marca Registrada. Bantam
Books, 666 Fifth Avenue, New York, New York 10103.*

PRINTED IN THE UNITED STATES OF AMERICA

CW   0 9 8 7 6 5 4 3

The Parent Game

CHAPTER

1

"Has anybody picked out their baby for the Family Living project yet?" asked Jana Morgan. The Fabulous Five, which included Jana, Christie Winchell, Beth Barry, Melanie Edwards, and Katie Shannon, were eating lunch together at their usual table in the cafeteria. They had been best friends for almost forever, and now they were in seventh grade at Wakeman Junior High, or Wacko, as most kids called it.

"Oh, I have mine!" chirped Melanie. "Did I tell you that Scott asked me to be a parent with him?"

"That's just so he can get you to change the diapers, make the formula, and do all the other work," interjected Katie. "Boys are all alike."

Melanie stuck out her tongue and made a disgusted face at her redheaded friend.

Jana wished she could get as excited as the others about the seventh-grade Family Living project. Mrs. Clark, her Family Living teacher, had said it was supposed to teach them something about the responsibilities of being a parent. Jana knew it had been tough for her own mother, who was divorced and trying to support the two of them on a low-paying job. Now Mrs. Morgan was getting married in two weeks, and Jana would be getting a stepfather. "Parent" was a big word in her life right now, and she definitely didn't feel like becoming one herself. In fact, she was wondering why she had brought up the subject with her friends in the first place.

For the project each student was supposed to choose a stuffed animal or toy and then treat it as if it were her or his own baby for two whole weeks. Everyone had to bring in the animal or toy for the teacher's approval on Wednesday, which was in two days. The make-believe child couldn't be left alone at any time or stuffed into a locker or have anything else done to it that wouldn't be done to a real baby. And when Mrs. Clark had explained that the baby even had to have diapers made out of old washcloths, or some other cloth, most of the boys had snickered and Richie Corrierro had held his nose.

As Jana tuned back into her friends' conversation, Christie was asking Melanie what her baby was going to be.

"A walrus."

Jana stared dumbfounded at Melanie, and she could see that her other friends were, too. Melanie was the most romantic girl in the world. Jana had expected something a little different for Melanie's baby.

"A *walrus*!" the four of them said in unison.

"Why in the world did you pick a *walrus*?" asked Jana.

"Yeah, yuck," said Beth, scrunching up her nose. "It has tusks and whiskers!"

"That's going to be some ugly baby," added Katie. "I'm not sure if it will look more like its mother or its father."

Melanie stuck out her tongue in Katie's direction again. "It's the idea that counts," she said huffily. "The walrus was Scott's when he was a baby, and I think it's *just precious*."

Katie put her face in her hands in despair.

"Jon and I are going to be make-believe parents together, too," said Christie. "We're going to use my bunny. You remember. It's the one that's dressed in a tennis outfit."

Jana saw a dreamy look come into Christie's eyes. Christie was the daughter of the principal of Mark Twain Elementary and was a whiz at nearly everything, especially math. Ever since she had tutored Jon Smith in math, and he had helped her in the seventh-grade elections for class president, they had been seeing a lot of each other.

"I haven't decided what I'm going to use," admitted Jana. "With the wedding so close, it's hard to keep my mind on school. I keep thinking about how *different* it's going to be at home after Mom and Pink are married."

"Well, I'm going to be a single parent," said Katie, as if she hadn't heard a word Jana had said about her mother's wedding or the worried sound in Jana's voice. "I'm not going to take care of a baby while some guy can play sports or whatever. Let them learn what being a parent is all about."

"Not all the boys are like that!" argued Melanie. She, too, seemed more interested in the parent project than in Jana's problems. "Scott would *never* leave me with *our* baby."

"You sound as if you're already married," responded Katie.

Jana shook her head. Melanie and Katie were constantly arguing over boys. Katie, the feminist of the group, was always accusing Melanie of being boy crazy, and Melanie, the romantic, was totally amazed that Katie had such low opinions of boys.

Jana listened to her friends talk. Normally she would be just as excited as they were over something as special as the parent project, but she had bigger worries now. Her mother was going to marry Pink, whose real name was Wallace Pinkerton, and Jana's life would change forever. It had seemed exciting at first. She had always wanted to be part of a real family. One with both a mother and a father. But the closer it got to the time for the wedding, the more doubts she had.

Pink was tall, blond, and nice looking and worked as a typesetter at the newspaper where her mother was classified ad manager, and they had been engaged for a long time. Mostly Pink came over on weekends, and he and her mother went bowling. It wasn't that Jana didn't like Pink. She really did. It was just that she and her mother had been alone together ever since her mother had divorced Jana's alcoholic father when she was three. Now with Pink's moving in, Jana felt as if she were being pushed into a little corner of their apartment, and even worse, a smaller corner of her mother's affection. All her mother could talk about lately was Pink, the wedding, and Jana's needing a new dress for the ceremony.

Jana glanced at her friends again. They had been excited when she first told them about the wedding, too. Especially Melanie, who always said that weddings were the most romantic things in the world. They had wanted to know every detail about her mother's dress, the wedding cake and the reception, all the fun stuff, but none of them seemed to know quite what to say when she tried to talk about how different things were going to be for her. None of them had ever been through an experience like it.

Jana sighed and stuffed her sandwich wrapper into her brown bag and got up. "See you guys later," she said halfheartedly.

Christie gave her a quick smile, and Beth waved with her fingers as she turned back to listen to Katie and Melanie argue.

"Hi." Randy Kirwan's voice startled Jana. She had been deep in thought when he caught up with her in the hall.

"Oh! Hi, back." His million-dollar smile seemed to brighten the hallway around them, and her spirits suddenly lifted. She had had a crush on Randy since fourth grade. He was the kindest and most sincere boy in the world, and had also been the handsomest in Mark Twain Elementary. They had kissed for the first time back in sixth grade, and now they were going together.

"Haven't seen you much lately. Been busy getting ready for the wedding?" he asked.

"Yes. My mother is totally frazzled. I never knew that there was so much work to getting married," she said with a laugh. "Besides that, Funny Hawthorne and I are working on the seventh-grade section of the yearbook. It's been taking lots of time. How about you?"

"Football practice and homework mostly."

"Have you chosen your baby yet for the Family Living class?" she asked. Jana wished Randy and she were in the same class so that they could be parents together, but unfortunately they weren't.

"Not yet, but I was thinking about asking Mrs. Blankenship if I can use my football. At least I know how to hold it. I've got no idea how to hold a baby." His blue eyes twinkled at her. "This is one class project I could really use help on."

"Oh, have you thought about getting a partner?" Jana was immediately sorry that she had asked. She didn't want to think about Randy's being a parent with someone else. She had just assumed he would be a single parent, and she would, too. It was sort of like showing everyone they were being true to each other.

"Are you volunteering for the job?" he asked with a sly grin.

"I can't, silly, but there are other girls in your class." And then she added quickly, "Mona Vaughn is in your class, isn't she?" Mona was nice, but she wasn't very pretty.

"Yes, she is. You know Taffy is in my class, too, and she's been talking about you a lot lately."

"She has?" Jana asked with surprise. Taffy had been her worst enemy at Mark Twain Elementary. Not too long ago they had even had clubs against each other.

"Yeah. She says how much she likes you. You two are really starting to be friends, aren't you?" Randy asked.

Jana remained silent, not knowing how to answer his puzzling question.

"I think that's great," Randy went on. "It always bothered me that you didn't get along at Mark Twain."

Jana swallowed hard. Randy always thought the best of people. "Yes, we are." What else could she say? Randy was such an honest and sincere person that he never realized all the horrible things that Taffy had done to her and The Fabulous Five back in Mark Twain. If Jana said Taffy was faking being nice, he might think that Jana was just being mean.

Jana hadn't seen much of Taffy since they had gotten to Wacko Junior High. In fact, The Fabulous Five were having a lot more trouble with Laura McCall and her clique, The Fantastic Foursome. They were from Riverfield Elementary and had become rivals of The Fabulous Five on the very first day at Wakeman Junior High.

But why would Taffy be telling Randy that she liked Jana? she thought as she called good-bye to Randy. Was it another one of Taffy's old tricks to steal Randy away from her?

CHAPTER

2

Jana stared with dismay at her reflection in the full-length mirror in the dressing room at Tanninger's Department Store after school. The dress just wasn't the right color for her. It didn't match her hair or her eyes or anything. And it was too childish looking. It wasn't something a girl in junior high school would wear. None of the dresses she had tried on in the young miss department looked good on her. Why did her mother insist on picking out such babyish things?

Behind her reflection she could see the hopeful look on her mother's face. Jana felt a momentary twinge of regret at her own lack of enthusiasm over finding a dress for the wedding. Her mother worked hard and barely made enough to support them.

Marrying Pink would probably make her mother's life a lot easier, and Jana supposed that she was in love with him.

Jana knew that her dad hadn't been a great husband. He hadn't been a very responsible father either. One summer he'd written to say that he would come and take her on a fabulous two-week vacation out west. Her mother had said she could go, and Jana had gotten all excited. She even wrote and told him she could hardly wait. But he never came. He didn't even write her to say why. She had thought it was her fault that he didn't want to see her until her mother told her that he had a problem. He was an alcoholic. Even though Jana hadn't seen him for a long time, she had never given up hope that someday she would open their apartment door and find him standing there. But now that would never happen because of Pink. He would be there instead.

It was going to feel really weird to have Pink coming home with her mother after work. Jana and her mother wouldn't be able to talk about things the vay they did now, sharing secrets and giggling over silly things. It would be totally different with him around. She would have to share her mother with Pink all the time, not just on weekends.

Jana blinked away the tears from her eyes and gave her mother's reflection a smile of encouragement.

"Well, honey, what do you think?"

"I don't know, Mom. It's just not right."

Jana saw her mother struggling to hide a look of

frustration. "We don't have a lot longer to find a dress and get it altered. The wedding is a week from Saturday."

"I know, but it's just not right. Can't we look some more?" she pleaded.

Her mother's shoulders sank slightly. "Sure."

Later in her room Jana sat cross-legged on her bed and went through her stuffed animals, trying to decide which one to use for class. She picked up Honeybear and held him to her face. He was a grubby-looking, brown-and-cream-colored bear that her mother said was Jana's favorite when she was a baby. She couldn't ever remember Honeybear's not being in the place of honor in front of the other animals piled against her pillows.

She hugged him tightly. At least he would still be her friend when Mom and Pink got married and her other friends were off doing their own things. No, she thought, Honeybear was too important to use in the Family Living class.

What about Turtle? Randy had won him for her at a carnival last summer, and she loved the dumb look on his face. He would make a funny-looking baby—almost as funny looking as Melanie's walrus, she'd bet. Still, with his fat middle and short legs he would be kind of hard to diaper. She had better not use him either, she decided.

Then there was the pink rabbit. Her father had sent that to her when she was four years old. She picked it up slowly from its place at the back of the pile and looked at it. She remembered deciding not to name it until her father came to visit and they could name it together. Since he hadn't come, it still didn't have a name. She put it down quickly, deciding instead to call one of her four best friends. That would lift her spirits.

Maybe she should call Beth first. The two of them had always been the best of friends and could really talk to each other. Beth was the dramatic one of The Fabulous Five. She was even in the Drama Club at school. The only problem that Beth had was she said some pretty wild things sometimes, and it always got her in trouble, such as the time she had tried to outbrag Laura McCall.

Jana smiled to herself. The Fabulous Five were always fun to be with. Back when they were in Mark Twain Elementary, they had meetings every Saturday in Jana's bedroom, and they would laugh and play records and plan things against Taffy Sinclair. Jana and her friends had even bought T-shirts that said The Fabulous Five across the fronts. Her friends had looked up to Jana as their leader, and she had to admit that it made her feel good.

Since they had been going to Wacko, they hadn't had enough time for their meetings. It seemed as if everyone always had something else to do. Just like Mom with Pink. Even though she had lots of new activities, too, Jana couldn't help wishing sometimes that things could be the same as they used to be.

She went into the living room and dialed Beth's number.

"Hello. TODD, STOP IT!" It sounded like Beth's younger sister, Alicia, shouting on the other end of the line. Her brother Todd must be trying to grab the phone away from her, Jana thought. In the background she could hear the Barry's sheepdog, Agatha, barking.

"Hi. This is Jana. Is Beth there?" Jana couldn't help shouting back.

"No, she's not. . . . *Quit it!* Can I take a message?"

"Uh, no." Jana hesitated. "That's all right. I'll call back later."

Melanie's line was busy. Jana waited five minutes and tried again but got only the *burrrp, burrrp* of the busy signal. Melanie could be talking to any one of several boys she currently had crushes on, thought Jana.

She dialed Christie's number next. Her mother told her that Christie and Jon were studying, but if it was important, she'd interrupt them. Jana told her not to.

Jana sighed. That left Katie. Or maybe she should call Randy. Thinking about Randy made little shivers of excitement run through her. Just the thought of his smiling face made her feel better.

The phone rang just as she reached for it. Her spirits leapt. Maybe it was Randy calling her!

"Hello, Jana?" The voice on the phone stopped her short.

"Yes."

"Jana, this is Taffy Sinclair. Do you have a few minutes to talk?"

Jana was immediately cautious. What was Taffy calling her about? They had always been mortal enemies, and they never talked to each other unless they absolutely had to.

"I've got something serious to talk to you about, and I wondered if you could come over," Taffy continued.

"What is it?" Jana asked suspiciously.

"I'd really rather not talk about it over the phone." Taffy paused and then added mysteriously, "It has something to do with Randy Kirwan."

Jana's mind whirled. Why would Taffy want to talk to her about Randy? Taffy had tried to steal Randy away from Jana several times in the past, but since they started junior high, Taffy hadn't been up to her old tricks. "What do you want to talk about Randy for?"

"Like I said, it's *too* important to talk about over the phone. *But* . . ."—she left the word hanging dramatically for a moment—"if you don't really want to know . . ."

"When should I come over?"

"Right now would be a good time."

Jana hesitated before saying, "I'll be right there." She looked at the receiver in her hand after Taffy had hung up. The steady drone of the dial tone sounded ominous.

CHAPTER

3

Jana stood on the front porch of Taffy's house waiting for someone to answer the door. Taffy lived in the nicer part of town, and it had taken Jana a full twenty minutes to bicycle over. She wouldn't have come for anything else that Taffy might have said except that she had something serious to talk about that concerned Randy Kirwan. It was just like Taffy to want to get Jana on her own turf without any of Jana's friends around.

It's funny, Jana thought, she'd known Taffy since the first grade, and the only time Taffy and she had come close to being friends was when they had found Baby Ashley in a basket on the front steps of Mark Twain Elementary. Baby Ashley had brought them close together for a short time, and Jana remembered the warm feelings they had shared as they knelt over the wiggling baby with her little hands waving and clutching at their fingers. It hadn't taken long, however, for Taffy to go back to being her old self and trying to hog the spotlight when the newspaper reporter came.

The door was opened by Taffy's mother. "Oh, hello, Jana."

"Hi, Mrs. Sinclair." If Jana could feel sorry for Taffy for any reason, it would be because of her mother. She was always pushing Taffy into acting and singing classes and modeling jobs, and she had even gotten her a role in one of the episodes of the TV show *Interns and Lovers*. Jana had to admit that Taffy had never looked better than in the death scene.

Jana stepped into the foyer as Taffy came into the living room. She couldn't believe it. Taffy was just as dressed up at home as she was at school. She was wearing a pleated skirt and a sweater layered over a gorgeous blouse, and her hair was pulled back with a bright blue ribbon. Seeing her made Jana feel scroungy in the old jeans she had put on after school.

"Hi, Jana," Taffy said, sweeping toward her.

"Hi," responded Jana, trying to be friendly in front of Taffy's mother.

"Let's go up to my room."

Upstairs Jana tried not to gawk. Taffy's room was big, like the rest of the rooms she had peeked into on their way, and it had been redecorated since the one other time Jana had been there. She had thought it was pretty then, but now she was sure it was the most beautiful bedroom she had ever seen. It was just as Jana imagined the bedrooms of movie stars would be. There was a silky canopy that had its center attached to the ceiling and fell in graceful folds to hide partially a large four-poster bed. In the middle was a pile of beautiful stuffed animals with the biggest white bear Jana had ever seen. It was dressed in a tutu and had a sparkly tiara on its head.

Everything was white in the room, including the furniture and the carpeting. Jana thought about her own little crowded bedroom with its used furniture in the tiny apartment she lived in with her mom. After Pink and her mother were married, she would probably even have to keep some of Pink's bowling trophies on the shelves in her room.

The walls of this room were covered with pictures of Taffy posing in different costumes. She was in gorgeous party dresses, sundresses, swimsuits, all kinds of beautiful things. Then there were pictures of Taffy with what looked like important people. She recognized some of them as movie stars; others looked as if they were just plain rich and important.

Jana was suddenly aware that Taffy was standing back while Jana admired her room. She was obviously eating up the chance to show off.

"Those are pictures taken by the studios I work for," Taffy said, moving to the wall with the most pictures on it. "This one was for Tanninger's spring catalog; that one was for a book cover—aren't those two boys standing on either side of me darling?"

She told Jana what each of the pictures was taken for. It impressed the socks off Jana, but she tried not to show it. She hadn't known that Taffy had done so much modeling.

"Mother's trying to get me a part in an after-school television show. It won't be very big, but it would be a start."

"Gee, that's great," said Jana. "You're getting to be really big-time."

Taffy smiled at the compliment. "It's just work, but it's starting to pay really well. Mother says I might even get a chance to go to Hollywood someday. She has dreams of my making it *really* big, and *her* having a beautiful home in Beverly Hills."

Jana thought she looked a little sad for a moment. Then Taffy brightened. "I really didn't ask you over to show you all my pictures. As I said on the phone, I have something serious to talk about.

"You know, Jana, you and I didn't get along at Mark Twain. You even had"—she hesitated and then corrected herself—"*we* even had clubs against each other. Since we've gotten to Wacko, though, we haven't really seen much of each other, and I've been thinking a lot about us." She had a worried look on her face. "I know you still have The Fabulous Five, but there's no reason for us to be enemies anymore."

It was as if Jana had been hit by a tidal wave. This

was not at all what she had expected to hear from Taffy Sinclair. She had assumed they would be enemies for life. "I guess not," she said hesitantly.

"To prove it, I want to do something for you, but I *won't* if you don't want me to. I promise."

Jana's old defensive instincts about Taffy came rushing back. What was she trying to pull?

"Randy and Laura McCall are in my Family Living class. I know how much you dislike Laura, kind of the way you felt about me in Mark Twain Elementary," she said with a sideways smile. "I heard Laura telling Tammy Lucero that she wanted to ask Randy Kirwan to be her partner in the parent project. I didn't think you would like that very much."

Jana stared blankly at Taffy. Randy and Laura McCall? Teaming up on the parent project? Her boyfriend and her worst enemy in junior high walking around school together and acting as if some stupid stuffed animal, or even Randy's *football*, was their darling little baby? Jana's face turned red as she realized just how much Laura would love to rub that in. She would absolutely die.

Taffy looked sympathetic. "Don't worry, Jana," she said as she gently placed a hand on Jana's arm. "I have a plan."

CHAPTER

4

*T*affy wants to help me? Jana thought in disbelief. It was impossible. They had *always* been enemies. It was true that they hadn't seen much of each other since they had come to Wakeman. She had been so busy getting used to junior high that Taffy hadn't been on her mind as much as she had been at Mark Twain Elementary. The Fantastic Foursome had taken her place as the number one enemy of The Fabulous Five. Still, Randy had said that Taffy had told him she liked Jana now.

"What kind of plan?" Jana asked. She braced herself to hear some obviously devious idea.

"I want you to remember that I won't do this if you say not to." Taffy seemed to be considering how to tell her. "I thought if *I* asked Randy to be *my* part-

21

ner on the Family Living project, Laura couldn't ask him, and then she couldn't steal him away from you. I'd only do it because I want us to be friends."

Jana felt as if she were going to be sick. Taffy and Randy acting as make-believe parents for two whole weeks? She didn't know whether to laugh or cry. How different would that be from Laura and Randy's being partners? she wondered. Was either one of the girls less likely to try to steal Randy away from her than the other?

Taffy did say she wanted to be friends, Jana reminded herself. And she wouldn't ask Randy to be partners if Jana didn't want her to. Did Taffy *really* want to be friends? Jana couldn't imagine going to Bumpers or to a movie with Taffy the way she did with The Fabulous Five. She felt trapped. What could she do?

"You have to decide real soon," Taffy said, gripping Jana's arm dramatically. "Laura may have already asked him." Jana thought the expression on Taffy's face must be right out of one of her acting classes.

"I don't know," Jana answered. She needed time to think. "This is awfully sudden. I don't know if I want to butt into something Randy is doing."

"I know you need time to think about it," Taffy said sweetly. "But Laura could ask him any minute. You've got to hurry and decide."

*   *   *

On the school ground the next morning Jana found Katie and Melanie waiting at their special place by the fence. Christie and Beth came up just as she was starting to repeat Taffy's offer.

"Don't tell me you believed her!" squealed Christie.

"I just can't figure out why she would lie to me," Jana answered defensively. "What can she gain? She could ask Randy to be a parent without even asking me, couldn't she? I couldn't do anything about that. And I'm certainly not going up to Randy and tell him he can't be Taffy's partner."

"You're right," said Katie. "That's what's so puzzling. But I just can't believe she'd do it out of the goodness of her heart."

"Maybe she *has* changed," said Melanie. "We haven't seen that much of her, and we certainly haven't had any fights with her lately."

"Taffy change?" asked Beth, rolling her eyeballs back in her head. "Not in a million years."

"So you haven't talked to Randy about it?" Christie asked.

"What would I say? Hey, Randy, don't be partners with Laura or Taffy on the Family Living project. They're just trying to steal you away from me. He'd think I was acting jealous."

"I guess so," agreed Christie. She seemed to be thinking the situation over. "I wonder if it *is* possible that Taffy feels differently about us," she said slowly. "Why don't we each try to talk to her and see how she reacts? You know, just make casual conversation. If she really feels differently about you, she ought to be friendly with all of us."

"Good idea," said Jana.

"Gosh," said Beth. "I don't think I can stand to go through life without Taffy Sinclair hating me."

Everyone laughed at that, and soon the conversation drifted back to the parent project.

"I can't wait to be parents with Scott," said Melanie. "It's going to seem just like we're married." She got the dreamy look in her eyes again.

"What about Shane Arrington and Garrett Boldt?" asked Christie. "I thought you liked them, too."

"I do, but Scott was my *first* true love. Then Shane was my second, and Garrett was my third."

The rest of The Fabulous Five giggled.

"I don't know how you can be so fickle," said Katie in an exasperated voice. "You act as if you want all the boys in Wacko Junior High for yourself."

"*Yeah*," answered Melanie. "But wouldn't it be fantastic? Besides, you're just saying that because Tony Calcaterra's not in your class."

This time Katie stuck *her* tongue out at Melanie.

"There's no one in my Family Living class that I want to team up with," said Beth.

"How about you, Jana?" Christie asked.

"Randy's not in my class, and I don't know if I want to team up with anyone else or not."

"Well, if you're going to object to Randy's teaming

up with someone, I don't think you should have a partner," said Beth.

"I'm not *against* Randy's being partners with someone. It's just who he teams up with, that's all." Then she added with a laugh, "Mona Vaughn would be fine."

"I guess so," said Christie. "She's not nearly as pretty as Taffy or Laura. But don't forget, Matt Zeboski is her boyfriend, and he's in that class, too."

"I heard that Laura is going to use a stuffed unicorn for a baby," Melanie continued.

"That's because it has a horn growing out of the top of its head and will look like her," said Beth, grinning widely at her own joke.

Katie said, "Lisa Snow told me she has a Garfield that she's going to use, and Tammy Lucero has an orange piñata that's shaped like a bull."

"Taffy's going to use a big white bear dressed in a tutu," said Jana. "She showed it to me last night. Is it ever gorgeous, and its name—get this—is Monique."

Just then the bell rang for class, and Jana followed behind the others. Marcie Bee called to her from two lockers away as they got their books out for class, "Oh, Jana! Doesn't the Family Living thing sound like fun?"

"Sure does," Jana answered.

"I've got the cutest bunny I've had for ages that I'm going to use. His name is Buniper. Of course I've got to put him through the wash and hang him out by his ears to dry before I can bring him in Monday."

"Great," responded Jana.

"I've got a kangaroo that I've had since I was a baby," said Dekeisha Adams, a tall black girl who was from Copper Beach Elementary. Jana knew Dekeisha from the modeling class they had been in at Tanninger's. She was also on the seventh-grade cheerleading squad with Beth and Melanie. "Its name is Jo-Jo. Won't that make a cute baby's name?"

Gloria Drexler and Melinda Thaler joined in the conversation as Jana pulled her books from her locker and left. Even though she was beginning to get more into the spirit of the parent project now that everyone else was excited and constantly talking about it, she couldn't get Taffy Sinclair out of her mind.

The morning took forever to pass. Jana had never been so bored with her classes, and she couldn't concentrate on what the teachers were saying. The more she thought about Taffy's offer, the more confused she became. Should she believe Taffy or not? Which would be worse, she wondered, to have Taffy as Randy's partner or Laura? One had been her worst enemy, and the other was probably her worst enemy now.

"Jana. Did you hear my question?" asked Miss Dickinson. "I asked you what your opinion is as to why the heroine behaved the way she did."

Perspiration popped out on Jana's forehead as she

suddenly remembered she was in her English Lit class. The last thing she remembered Miss Dickinson talking about was the book she had assigned the class to read.

Jana struggled to remember the story. She hoped it was the heroine in the book that Miss Dickinson was asking about. She gulped and said, "Uh, she did it because she felt that no one loved her. Uh . . . she was trying to get attention."

"Very good, Jana. Please pay attention. Now class . . ."

Jana's thoughts went immediately back to Randy, Taffy, and Laura. What *was* she going to do?

CHAPTER

5

Several students were in the yearbook staff room when Jana arrived after school. Mr. Neal was looking at photographs with Garrett Boldt, and other students were working in groups of twos and threes.

Jana loved the busy atmosphere in the room. Large sheets of paper with lists of things for each of the classes to do and schedules for photo sessions were taped all around the walls. There were personal computers on some of the tables and piles of paper and things they needed to prepare *The Wigwam*. It seemed so businesslike, just like a newsroom.

"Hi, Jana!" Funny called. Funny Hawthorne was one of the members of The Fantastic Foursome clique, and the only *good* one as far as Jana was concerned.

Laura McCall was their leader. It was even rumored that she made her friends do certain things to remain members of The Fantastic Foursome. Melissa McConnell was the fastidious one. She was precise in every way and had run against Christie for seventh-grade president, probably at Laura's insistence. Tammy Lucero was the world's biggest gossip. But Jana and Funny had hit it off from their very first day at Wacko Junior High when Funny returned the class schedule that Jana had dropped. Lots of people thought Funny was a bubblehead, but she really wasn't. She just had a great sense of humor and showed it by laughing a lot.

"How are the plans coming for your mom's wedding?" Funny asked, beaming at Jana with her usual big smile.

"Okay, I guess. But Mom's turning into a basket case. I can't believe how she's worrying about every little detail as if the world will come to an end if even the smallest thing goes wrong. I guess she's just nervous, but I hope I'm not like that when I get married." Jana rolled her eyes toward the ceiling and then grinned at Funny, who sat at a table covered with papers. "So, what are you up to?"

"I got started on the list of committees and other activities that seventh-graders are in. Do you want to help?"

"Sure," said Jana, dragging over a chair. Being around Funny always lifted her spirits. "What do you have so far?"

"I've got the football team and the boys' and girls' basketball teams. Then there are the track teams and soccer. Of course there's the class officers. We need *b-i-i-g* pictures of them. That way, you and I get our pictures in special." She giggled.

"Don't forget the Teen Court," said Jana.

"Oh, that's right. Your friend Katie's on that, isn't she?"

Funny looked down when she said that. Jana wished it were easier for the two of them to be friends. Even though they belonged to separate cliques that were always at war with each other, they each understood how the other one felt. That helped a lot, but Jana had seen Funny and Laura arguing once, and she knew it was because Funny was hanging around Jana.

"Yes, Katie's on it, and so are Shane Arrington and Whitney Larkin," Jana answered.

Funny continued with her list of activities. "And then there's the Drama Club and the cheerleading squad and the band."

"There sure are a lot of seventh-graders doing things," said Jana. "Let's see, on cheerleading there's Mandy McDermott, Dekeisha Adams, Melanie, and Beth and . . . oh, yes, Laura. Sorry. I almost forgot her. I didn't do it on purpose." She gave Funny a look that said she truly was sorry.

"You know," said Funny thoughtfully, "Laura really isn't all that bad. You guys have the wrong idea about her."

Jana didn't answer right away, although she knew Funny was waiting for her to say something. After thinking for a moment she said, "I know you Fantastic Foursomes are all friends, just the way we are in The Fabulous Five. But it sure seems as if Laura's out to get us."

Funny was silent herself for a moment. "It seems the other way around, too." Then she touched Jana's arm. "You're the leader of The Fabulous Five. They'll do whatever you want. Isn't there some way you can make them understand?"

Jana looked at Funny. "I heard that Laura is going to ask Randy Kirwan to be her partner for the Family Living project. Is that true?"

A cloud passed over Funny's face, and she said quietly, "She did say she wished he would ask her." Then she added quickly, "But she said she'd like to be Shane's partner, too, except that he's not in her class."

"I know," said Jana. "Shane's in Mrs. Clark's Family Living class with me."

"Well," said Funny, looking sad, "I guess we'd better work on this list."

Jana hurried into Bumpers. Funny and she had made lists of most of the activities that seventh-graders were involved in and had put down the names of all the kids they could think of who were doing things. She had finally told Funny she had mentioned to Randy that she would meet him, and she had to leave early. They each took half the names of the kids to call to make sure they were at the photo sessions.

Bumpers was full, as usual. Every booth, table, and bumper car was crowded with Wacko Junior High kids. Melanie, Christie, Beth, and Katie were squeezed together in a booth with Mona Vaughn and Sara Sawyer. Taffy was sitting with Lisa Snow and Kim Baxter. Laura McCall, Tammy Lucero, and Melissa McConnell were by the counter talking to Shane Arrington and Tony Sanchez. Jana's friends in The Fabulous Five waved when they saw her come in.

"See if you can get a chair," called Christie.

"Don't," said Sara. "I want to go talk to Stacy and Gloria, so you can have my seat."

"I'll go with you," volunteered Mona.

"How's the yearbook coming?" asked Katie as Jana slid into the booth.

"Fine. Funny and I are working on the lists of activities that seventh-graders are on. We've got all of your names down."

"Just think. Someday *The Wigwam* will probably be valuable because my picture is in it," said Beth. "I can see it now. Former student of Wacko Junior High makes Broadway. They might even change the name of the school to Beth Barry Junior High. Wouldn't that be neat?"

"Dream on," said Katie. I'll bet they rename it

after that famous female Supreme Court justice."

"Why do you think they would name it after Sandra Day O'Connor?" asked Melanie.

"Not her. I'm talking about me—Her Honor, Katie Shannon," said Katie. The others groaned loudly.

"Save my seat while I get a soda," Jana said, digging her change purse out of her pocketbook.

She was standing in line waiting to order when Taffy came up behind her. "Hi, Jana." Jana almost jumped with surprise. She had been avoiding Taffy because she didn't want to be pushed for an answer about Taffy and Randy's being partners. She just hadn't figured out Taffy's motive yet.

"Hi," she answered.

"See that gorgeous guy over there?" asked Taffy, speaking in confidential tones and nodding toward a group of boys. "The one wearing the pullover shirt with green stripes?"

Jana knew who he was, but she had never spoken to him. He was Chad Wallace, and everyone thought he was the biggest deal in the eighth grade. He played all the sports and was even on the varsity team. He was even a bigger deal than Garrett Boldt. "Sure. What about him?" she asked.

"I think he's *really cute*. He even spoke to me the other day. He's been looking at me, and I think he's about to ask me out."

"Really?" said Jana. "But he's in eighth grade."

"I know. But I like older men," Taffy said with a

confiding grin. "Don't tell anyone, but right now *he's all I want in the world*."

"He is?"

"Sure. Isn't he gorgeous?"

Jana looked over at Chad. He was certainly handsome. He was almost as good-looking as Randy, except a little older. "That's nice, Taffy. I hope he does ask you out."

"Me, too. Oh, I think I've changed my mind. I was going to get some french fries, but they're fattening. See you later, Jana."

Jana watched Taffy walk away. That was weird. Taffy had certainly never confided in her about boys before. Maybe she did want to be friends, after all.

"We saw you talking to Taffy," Christie said. "Was she trying to tell you again what a great friend she is?"

"Not really. She was telling me how much she likes Chad Wallace."

"Chad Wallace? He's neat!" said Melanie.

"Taffy said she's wild about him, and she thinks he's going to ask her out. Did any of you see her at school?" asked Jana.

"I did," answered Beth.

"Was she friendly?"

"She was as sweet as can be. I nearly threw up."

"I saw her, too," said Christie. "And she was nice to me, also."

"I saw her, but I couldn't bring myself to talk to her," said Katie.

"It looks as if she might just be serious about wanting to be friends," Jana said, thinking out loud.

"There you go, being trusting again," warned Katie.

"Well, she is acting differently. She said she wouldn't ask Randy to be her partner unless I said okay, and Randy said she's been talking about how much she likes me. And don't forget, she was nice to you guys. Now she says she's crazy about Chad Wallace. Maybe she *is* telling the truth."

"Have you found out who Randy wants for a partner?" Beth asked Jana. She nodded toward the booth where he was sitting with Scott Daly, Keith Masterson, and Bill Soliday.

"I asked him yesterday, but I didn't find out anything. Maybe I'll try again."

"I could go over and tell him to come to our booth because you want to talk to him," suggested Melanie.

"I'd be embarrassed. I'm not going to talk to him about whether he is going to be partners with someone in here in front of everyone."

"If you wait until later, we won't know what he said until tomorrow," complained Melanie. "You'd have to call us."

"Look!" Katie said, putting out her hands to silence them. "He's going to the jukebox. Maybe you can ask him now."

"Yeah, go ahead," said Christie, practically pushing Jana out of the booth. "This is your chance."

Jana summoned up all her courage and wove her way across the room to meet Randy at the old Wurlitzer jukebox.

"Hi," she said stopping beside him at the machine.

"Hi, back," he said, reaching out and putting an arm around her waist. "Do you have a song you want to hear?"

She looked down at the rows of song titles. "Number B-eight."

"Great. That's my favorite, too."

Okay. Here goes, Jana thought, taking a deep breath. "You never told me if you were going to have a partner for the Family Living project," she said, trying her best to sound casual.

He was just about to answer when Laura McCall's voice came from behind them. "Hi, Randy. Are you going to play a song for me?" she asked.

"Hi, Laura," answered Randy. "What would you like to hear?"

"Whatever you like, I'd like." She gave Jana a hostile smile as she flicked her long blond braid with one hand.

Jana glared at her. "I think I'd also like to hear number H-twenty-three," Jana said to Randy. "Remember how we used to listen to it when we went to Mama Mia's Pizzeria after the Mark Twain football games?"

Randy smiled at her and turned back to look at the song titles. Jana inched closer to him, sticking her shoulder in front of Laura.

"Oh, how cute, Jana. You still like grade school things." Her voice dripped sugar.

Jana fumed. "Some people just establish relationships that last and super memories to go with them," she said through clenched teeth. Randy seemed unaware of the war that was going on right next to him as he punched number H-twenty-three.

"What did you ask me about school before?" he asked Jana.

"Uh . . . I forgot." She couldn't talk about the Family Living project with Laura standing right there.

"Hey, Randy," yelled Scott from across the room. "Keith says there's no way you can run the one-hundred-yard dash in ten point two seconds."

"That's all he knows," Randy yelled back. "Excuse me," he said to Jana and Laura. "I've got to straighten this guy out."

He left Jana and Laura standing together. Laura looked at Jana and then spun around, whipping her braid across Jana's arm.

"The nerve of her," said Katie when Jana sat down again with her friends. "How could she push in on you and Randy like that while you were talking?"

"Boy, that witch butted right in," huffed Christie.

"You should have punched her out," advised Melanie.

"What did Randy say?" asked Beth. "Did you get to talk to him about the project at all?"

"He was just about to tell me about it when Laura pushed her way in," answered Jana.

"So you still don't know if he's going to team up with anyone?" asked Katie.

"No. But one thing's for sure. Laura will be his partner over my dead body." Out of the corner of her eye Jana could see Taffy looking at her.

CHAPTER

6

*R*andy took Jana's hand as they walked home from Bumpers. He had come up to her as she was leaving and had taken her books from her. It made her tingle when he held her hand in his.

"Are you coming to the game Saturday?" he asked.

"I'm not sure. I want to, but my mother has been bugging me to go shopping for a dress for her and Pink's wedding. I think I can still get there, though."

"Hey, I'd forgotten about the wedding. It's getting pretty close, isn't it? Are you going to be a bridesmaid?" he asked.

"I'm going to be maid of honor. I do need a dress for the wedding, but I'm so busy."

Randy looked down at her as they walked along.

"The wedding must be pretty important to your mom."

"I know," Jana murmured. She felt uncomfortable with him looking at her. She was busy and couldn't help it if she didn't have time to shop for the dress. Besides, just thinking about the wedding made her feel strange.

She forced herself to smile as they walked on hand in hand under the tall maple trees that arched over the sidewalk of her street. When they reached the porch of her apartment building, she leaned back against the pillar, not wanting to say good-bye to him yet. She still hadn't found out what he was planning to do about the parent project.

"I hope you can get your shopping done and come to the game Saturday," he said, a serious look on his face. "I play better when you're there, and Trumbull Junior High can be tough."

The look on his face sent a thrill through her, and he leaned forward and kissed her forehead. Suddenly the feeling of anxiety washed back over her.

"Have you decided whether you're going to be partners with anyone yet?" she asked quickly.

"No. I was thinking about being a single parent, but Laura McCall was talking about how much easier the project would be with a partner. I think she's right."

Jana's body went rigid. "Did she ask you to be partners with her?"

"No. Some of us in Mrs. Blankenship's class were just talking."

Jana felt her muscles relax. Laura *was* about to ask Randy, she just knew it. She had to talk to Taffy right away.

"Why don't we go out to the mall and look for your dress after we clean up the dishes?" Jana's mother asked at the dinner table. "It's such a nice evening it would be good to get out. Maybe we'll go to a movie afterward." Jana knew the movie was just an enticement to get her to look for a dress.

"Actually, Mom, tonight isn't good. I've got homework and I'm supposed to call a lot of the kids that haven't come in yet to sign up for their yearbook pictures." Besides those reasons, thought Jana, Taffy hadn't been home when she called her house. Her mother had said she would ask Taffy to call when she got home. Jana had to talk to her tonight.

The smile faded from her mother's face. "What about tomorrow evening then?"

"I don't know. It depends on how many of the kids I reach this evening, I guess."

"When do they have to have their pictures taken by?"

"Oh, before December."

"That's a long time away, sweetheart. Couldn't you wait to call some of them?"

"It's not so long when you've got nearly two hundred kids who have to get their pictures taken," Jana said.

"You know, the wedding is a lot closer than December, and we have just *got* to get you a dress. It might have to be altered. Couldn't you put off some of your calling one evening so we can go out to the mall?"

There she goes, getting paranoid again, Jana thought, stirring her lasagna with her fork. "I guess so."

Her mother pursed her lips and frowned. Jana tried to ignore the look of frustration. She knew the wedding was getting closer, but you couldn't just ignore everything else. The yearbook was a big thing, and there were so many things to do to get it ready for publication. Her mother didn't understand. And she *had* to talk to Taffy. If her mother would *just* quit mentioning the dress, Jana would find time to shop for it.

After dinner, as Jana went to her room to get her list of kids to call, she heard the phone ring.

"Jana! Telephone," her mother called. She went back to the kitchen and picked up the receiver. "Hello."

"Jana?" It was Taffy.

"Oh, Taffy. I'm glad it's you. I wanted to talk to you about your being partners with Randy for the Family Living class."

"Yes?"

"It's just for the class, isn't it?"

"Of course it is. Sometime you can return the favor. Like when I have a modeling appointment or an acting class and it's my turn to take care of Randy's and my baby, you could sit for me. You *would* do that, wouldn't you?"

The words *Randy's and my baby* echoed in Jana's ears. She hated the way they sounded coming from Taffy. At least Taffy had pointed Chad out to her at Bumpers and said she was crazy about him. If she was as crazy about Chad as she said, she couldn't be out to steal Randy.

"Sure, Taffy. Anytime. Just let me know."

"I will."

By the time she hung up the receiver, Jana was feeling a lot better. With Taffy's help she would show Laura McCall that she couldn't steal Randy. She went back to her room with a smile on her face. She would choose her baby now and then call some kids about getting their pictures taken. The Family Living project was going to be fun, after all.

CHAPTER

7

*J*ana hurried to school the next morning. She held
her books in one arm and in the other hand carried
a brown grocery bag containing her make-believe
baby. It was okay to carry it that way until next
week, after it was approved by the teacher and became an *official* baby. All around the grounds were
seventh-graders carrying bags and boxes and stuffed
animals.

"Hi," called Dekeisha Adams. She was carrying a
big kangaroo and walking with Marcie Bee, who had
a clear plastic cleaning bag with a rabbit in it slung
over one shoulder.

"Hi, Dekeisha. Did you wash Buniper, Marcie?"
Jana called.

"Yes, and I hung him on the line by his ears to dry

and they stretched three inches." Marcie sounded exasperated. "Now they won't stand up."

"Why don't you tie them in a bow and tell everyone Buniper is a girl?" Jana asked with a laugh.

"Good idea."

Katie, Christie, Beth, and Melanie were already at their special place by the fence.

"Oh, no, Melanie!" cried Jana as she stepped up. "Is *that* your baby?"

Melanie was holding a gray walrus with saggy skin and white tusks. Black whiskers stuck out from both sides of its nose. "Don't laugh," she warned. "Everyone else has been making fun of me since I got here."

"Why isn't Scott carrying it?" asked Jana. "It's his—isn't it?"

"He wanted to go to the Quick Stop for a slushy with Matt Zeboski, and he asked me if I'd hold it."

"I told you," said Katie. "Boys will have you doing all the work. That's why I'm going to be a single parent."

"Just because I'm doing it this once, doesn't mean I'm going to do it all the time," said Melanie, glaring at Katie.

"Right," said Katie with a cynical look on her face.

"Well, I don't think that Sheena doll you're carrying is such a cute baby either," Melanie shot back.

"It's the only thing I could get away from Libber. That cat sleeps with all my animals and toys."

"Your bunny in the tennis outfit is cute, Christie," said Jana.

"My dad gave it to me when I was little. I think he thought I'd be a better tennis player if I kept it near me."

"What's in your bag, Jana?" asked Beth.

Jana opened it and held out the sides so her friends could see. In it was the pink bunny with no name her father had given her when she was a baby.

"Quiet down, class," said Mrs. Clark. "It's time to check your choices for babies. Why don't we start with you, Whitney? Will you show us your child?"

Whitney Larkin, who was a brain and had skipped sixth grade at Copper Beach Elementary and come straight to junior high this year, stood up. "Curtis Trowbridge and I have decided to be make-believe parents together, and we have chosen this robot to be our baby," she said, as if she were reciting an algebra formula.

She held it up for the class to see. The plastic toy looked like something out of a science fiction movie. Whitney punched a button and a red light moved behind its visor, and then it started walking around the floor. Jana looked at Curtis, who was beaming like a proud new father. Curtis, who had gone to Mark Twain Elementary with her and was the nerd of the world, had been walking through the halls holding hands with Whitney ever since school began. They're the perfect couple if there ever was one, thought Jana, and they couldn't have picked a better child.

"Hmm, it's certainly different, but I see no reason why you can't use it, Whitney and Curtis. Very good. All right, Clarence Marshall, what have you chosen for your baby?"

"This mouse," said Clarence, holding up a small, gray, hairy mouse for everyone to see. He squeezed it and it went *Squeak! Squeak!* The rest of the class broke up laughing.

Mrs. Clark frowned but finally she said Clarence could use the mouse. He stuck it back in his jeans pocket.

Each of the students took turns showing their make-believe babies. When it was her turn, Jana took the rabbit from the bag and was about to show it. Clarence Marshall, who was seated in front of her, twisted around to see.

Squeak! Squeak!

"Clarence, don't hurt your baby!" yelled Joel Murphy.

"Mouse abuse!" yelled Shane. The whole class started yelling at Clarence not to hurt his baby.

Clarence grinned as he dug into his pocket and pulled the mouse out by its head.

"Clarence, next week you'll have to treat it better," scolded Mrs. Clark. "Think of it as a child. Class"— she looked at everyone as she spoke—"I want you all to understand that this is to be taken *seriously*. If *any-*

thing happens to the toy or stuffed animal that you have chosen, you could fail the course. You are responsible for it and *must* follow the rules and keep a detailed schedule of feedings, bedtimes, and so forth. If you have chosen to be partners with someone else, it's up to *both of you* to make sure it is taken care of properly, or you *both* could fail. You can get a sitter for your child, but it cannot be one of your parents. Is that perfectly clear?" The room was so quiet you could hear a pin drop. Jana smiled to herself as she saw Clarence lay his mouse very carefully on a tissue as if it were a tiny bed.

"All right, let's continue. Shane, what do you have in the box?"

Jana had been wondering about the box ever since Shane had brought it into the classroom. It had two or three holes punched into it on each side.

Shane untied the string and gently reached into the box. Out came a large iguana with its legs and tail protruding through a small diaper. Its tongue flicked out at Mrs. Clark, and she pulled back in surprise.

"IGOR!" everyone in the class shouted. "*It's Igor!*"

Jana threw her head back and laughed as everyone in the room shrieked at the sight of Shane's pet lizard. I should have guessed that Shane would try to use Igor as his baby, she thought.

Mrs. Clark was struggling to regain her composure. "Shane Arrington, what is that?"

"It's Igor," said Shane with a cool smile. "He's my iguana."

"Humph!" Mrs. Clark said softly. "Live animals are *not* to be used in the Family Living project, Shane. You will just have to choose something else."

"Gee. He really wanted to be a part of it," said Shane. Then he spoke to the lizard. "Sorry, old buddy. I told you it wouldn't work."

As they were leaving class, Shane came up to Jana. "Hey, Jana. Would you like to be partners?"

"Partners?" Jana echoed in surprise. Being partners with Shane would probably be lots of fun, and now that Randy was going to be partners with Taffy, it was probably all right if she had a partner, too. "I guess so," she said, "but only if we don't use Igor, as Mrs. Clark said. And . . . ," she added, remembering what Katie had been telling Melanie about boys trying to get out of all the work, "if I don't have to take care of it all the time."

"That's cool," he answered. "I believe in equal opportunity. Remember my folks were liberated a long time ago."

Jana knew his mother and father had been hippies in the sixties and still wore beaded headbands and patched jeans, so it was probably true.

"When I'm playing football, you can take care of them, and when you're working on the yearbook, I'll take care of them. Otherwise we'll switch off evenly."

"That sounds okay." A warning bell went off inside her head. *"Them?* But Mrs. Clark said Igor can't be used."

"I know," Shane replied with a grin. "But I thought it would still be fun to have a boy and a girl. Your bunny can be the girl, and my dinosaur can be the boy."

"Dinosaur?" asked Jana incredulously.

"Sure. Don't worry. He's stuffed. I asked Mrs. Clark about him just now, and she said okay."

Jana smiled weakly and headed for her next class. Oh, brother, she thought. First Igor and now a dinosaur. What am I getting myself into?

CHAPTER

8

*J*ana wadded the sheet of stationery into a ball and threw it into the wastebasket next to her desk. The pink bunny her father had given her sat on the desktop in front of her, and Rex, Shane's dinosaur, was in the chair next to her bed. He had said that he'd named it Rex because that's what it was—a Tyrannosaurus rex.

The whole thing seemed like a story out of a little kids' picture book to Jana. Both of the stuffed animals were dressed in makeshift diapers she had made from clean dustcloths, and they had soda bottles with rubber nipples on them filled with the make-believe formula that she had prepared. She had even filled out the schedule on their feedings and things.

What made it even more weird was the way Rex looked. Rex was the biggest stuffed animal Jana had ever seen. He was green with a purple belly and a yellow tuft of hair sticking up from the center of his head, and the wacky look on his face was positively stupid.

Jana shook her head in disbelief at the dinosaur and pulled another sheet of stationery from the desk drawer. She tried starting the letter for the third time.

> *Dear Father:*
> *I am writing this letter to tell you about Mom and Pink's wedding. I am sure you will be just as happy about it as I am.*

Jana paused and looked at what she had written. Did it still seem too formal? Or was it too casual? She didn't want him to think that she was dying to see him, because she wasn't. But she also didn't want him to think that she hated him, because she didn't think she did. She didn't really know how she felt—about him, about Pink, about the wedding, about *any* of it—but she knew someone should let him know about the wedding.

> *Pink is a very nice man.*

Would her father think she meant that *he* wasn't a

nice man? She crossed out the last sentence and thought for a moment.

> *It will be nice to have a man around the house to help Mom with things.*

If he thought that was a slam about his not being around, well, he could just think it. He hadn't even come the one time he had written to say that he would.

> *They are getting married one week from Saturday.*

Would he think that was an invitation for him to come to the wedding? No, of course he wouldn't. Children of people getting married didn't send out invitations. She didn't know if he even cared that her mother, his ex-wife, was getting married. He hadn't cared enough to keep up the alimony and child support payments, and her mother had quit trying to collect them a long time ago. There had been times when her mother sat at the kitchen table with the bills, and Jana knew she was worrying about having the money to pay them. Why should he start caring now? Why was she even writing the letter to him anyway?

She leaned back in her chair and stared at the ceiling. Probably for the same reason that I keep putting off getting my dress, she thought. It was hard to admit it to herself, but she knew that getting the dress would mean that everything was set. All the details were taken care of, and the wedding would take place. That was okay for her mom. In fact, it was super for her.

"But what about me?" she whispered. Just as tears started to well up in her eyes, she was aware of Rex, smiling at her from his chair.

Jana glanced at the green and purple dinosaur again and smiled back at him, in spite of herself. Shane had said that Rex was the only stuffed animal his parents had given him as a baby. He said for a long time he had thought Rex was his big brother. He was only kidding of course, although Melanie, who was with them at the time, had believed him.

Her thoughts went back to the letter. What else should she say to her father? How are things going? I'd like to see you sometime?

"Jana?" her mother spoke from the doorway.

Jana slid her school notebook over the letter. "Oh, hi," she answered stiffly.

"May I come in?"

"Sure."

"What are you doing, sweetheart?"

"Just my homework."

"My, that's a big dinosaur. Where did you get that?"

"It belongs to Shane Arrington. It's a Tyranno-saurus rex, and it's supposed to be one of our make-believe babies for the Family Living project. We decided to have a boy and a girl."

"Oh, I see," said her mother, chuckling as she looked Rex over. "And your rabbit is the other baby?"

Jana nodded and wished she had not put the bunny her father had given her where her mother could see it.

"Do you have a minute to talk, Jana?" she continued. "We just have to set a time to find you a dress. Since evenings are out, and we talked about Saturday, can we make it definite?"

Jana shrugged as the old feelings of resistance returned. If she could just put off shopping for a dress until she got her feelings sorted out. "Now I've got the problem of what to do with Rex," she offered hopefully.

"Rex?"

"Yes, the dinosaur. That's what Shane named him. I can't leave him and my bunny alone, and he's almost too big to lug around the mall."

Her mother stared at the stuffed animals. Rex seemed to be smiling back at her with his idiot grin. "You can't leave them at home?"

"No, not without someone to sit them. That's one of the rules. Remember? I told you about it," she said sharply, and then wished she could bite her tongue. Her mother was so preoccupied with the wedding that she couldn't concentrate on anything else. "You can leave them with a sitter, but it can't be a parent," she explained patiently. "If I did and Mrs. Clark found out, I could get an F on the project."

"Can't you get Shane to take care of them?"

"Oh, he will, but I said I'd take care of them when he's playing football, and he'll take care of them when I'm working on the yearbook. The other times we'll take turns. There's a game with Trumbull Saturday afternoon."

Her mother looked frustrated again. "Jana, we have just *got* to get you a dress. Can't one of your friends sit for you?"

"They'll all be at the game, and they've talked everyone who isn't going into sitting for them."

"Well," her mother sighed, "we'll just have to take your babies shopping with us."

"But Rex is so *big*."

"Jana, don't you *want* to get a new dress for the wedding?"

Jana ducked her head so that her mother couldn't see the expression on her face. "Sure I do, Mom. It's just that I've got problems." Why couldn't she understand? "I'm not doing it on purpose."

Jana's mother looked at her. "Jana, honey, don't you like Pink anymore?"

Jana looked at her in astonishment. "Of course I do."

"Well, the way you're acting, I'm beginning to wonder."

"The way I'm acting? I just have school things that I *have* to do, and now I have to take care of

Shane's dumb dinosaur. I didn't invent them. They have nothing to do with Pink."

"Well, young lady, we're going shopping Saturday morning for a dress, and that's final." Sparks flew out of her mother's eyes. "We'll just have to manage to do it *with* the animals." She stood up and looked down at Jana.

Jana fought back tears. "Okay," she said weakly. Her mother turned and left abruptly.

As the door closed, the tears gushed and spilled down Jana's cheeks. Her mother hadn't spoken to her like that since she was a little kid and had done something naughty. And now she felt as if she were being treated as if she were a little kid again.

She took the unfinished letter from under the notebook and wadded it up and threw it at the pink rabbit. It bounced and ended up on the floor. She stared at it for a few moments, then got up and retrieved it. She spread it flat on the desktop and tried to press the wrinkles out of it. A tear splashed on the paper and made the ink run. Why couldn't her mother understand?

CHAPTER

9

"Wow, Jana, are you so lucky! It's not every girl who gets a chance to be maid of honor at her own mother's wedding." Christie was holding her bunny and was grinning from ear to ear.

Jana couldn't help smiling to herself. It must have been the millionth time one of her friends had said that.

The Fabulous Five were standing by the fence, and Jana had her pink bunny in one arm and her books in the other. Rex was sitting on the ground next to her. He was so big that he came almost up to her waist. His eyes, which were made of plastic with loose black spots in them, were crossed, making him look dumber than ever. Melanie had Scott's walrus, Beth had her panda bear that looked raggedy because her dog, Agatha, had chewed on it. And Katie was carrying her Sheena doll. All of the make-believe babies had on diapers made out of assorted cloths.

"And think of all the flowers and beautiful music and the wedding vows. I get weepy thinking about it," said Beth. "It will be a church wedding, won't it?"

"I think they should go on a honeymoon," said Melanie before Jana could answer. "Maybe to Hawaii. It's *sooo* romantic there."

"Have they signed a prenuptial contract?" asked Katie. "Will your mother keep a separate bank account? I don't think it's wise to mix all the money. It allows the man to take control, if you're not careful."

"Of course I'm excited," answered Jana. "And they can't really afford to go on a honeymoon. It will be a small church wedding. And I don't think they've signed any contract, Katie. Not everyone thinks like you do."

"Well, it pays to be safe. After you're married it's too late."

"Look who's talking as if she's been married a zillion times and knows all about what to do," Christie countered.

"The way you talk, Katie," added Melanie, "it sounds as if marriage is a war."

"Have you gotten your dress yet?" asked Beth, and Jana felt sure she was changing the subject before the argument between Katie and Melanie got out of hand.

"Not yet," she admitted. "I guess I keep putting it off. It's going to seem really strange to have Pink as a permanent member of the family."

"It'll be okay," said Beth, putting a reassuring hand on Jana's arm. "Just think how long you've known him. It isn't as if he's a stranger, or anything."

Jana nodded. "You're right." She tried to sound confident, but she could feel her chin begin to quiver. Quickly she added, "Anyway, we're going shopping for my dress on Saturday before the game. Would any of you guys like to sit with a dinosaur and a bunny while I go shopping?"

"He's cute," said Melanie, running her fingers through the shock of yellow hair that stuck straight up from Rex's head. "Anything Shane has would have to be darling."

"I'm afraid I'm busy," said Katie.

"Me, too," added Beth, and the others nodded.

"Oh, well," said Jana with a shrug. "Thanks anyway."

"Hey, I thought you were going to send us invitations to the wedding," said Christie. "I haven't gotten mine yet."

"Me, either," said Melanie.

Beth and Katie joined in the chorus asking Jana what had happened to their invitations to the wedding.

"Eeek!" said Jana. "I was so busy with the parent project and the yearbook that I forgot to send them. I'll get them out tonight. I promise."

"Look over there," said Katie.

Taffy Sinclair was coming onto the school ground next to Chad Wallace, and she was carrying the big white bear in the tutu that Jana had seen on her bed. They had barely walked through the gate when Chad saw Garrett Boldt and two other eighth-grade boys and left Taffy standing alone. She looked around, saw The Fabulous Five, and headed for them with a huge grin on her face.

"Hi, Jana, Melanie, Beth, Katie, and Christie," Taffy said, smiling so big that she was showing her crooked bicuspid. "Oooh, it takes a lot of breath to say all your names at one time. Maybe I should just say 'The Fabulous Five.'" She smiled sweetly, and there was an excited sound in her voice.

Taffy continued, "Did you see me with Chad Wallace? Can you *believe* he walked me to school? He tried to make it look as if he ran into me by accident, but *I* think he was waiting for me." She looked at Jana as she spoke as if she especially wanted her to hear.

"That's really something, Taffy," said Jana. "Most eighth-grade boys ignore seventh-grade girls."

"Garrett Boldt is interested in me," interjected Melanie. "He almost asked me out."

"Oh, Jana," Taffy said, as if it were an afterthought. "I talked to Randy. He said he would be my partner on the Family Living project. Now Laura can't steal him from you. Let me know if there's *anything* else I can do for you. I'll be glad to," she said, smiling sweetly. "That's what friends are for. Well, I've got to turn in some homework. I'll see you girls later. Maybe we can eat lunch together. Bye, bye."

The Fabulous Five stared after her. "She wants to eat lunch with us," said Katie. "I never thought I'd hear her say that."

"Me, either," agreed Beth. "And she said, *helping friends is what friends are for.* Can you believe it?"

"Hey, look, guys," said Christie. "People do change, you know. Maybe even Taffy can."

"She has been acting differently lately," admitted Jana. "She did fix it so Laura McCall can't be Randy's partner. She was walking with Chad Wallace, so she must be interested in him and not Randy." Katie looked doubtful. "Katie, you don't trust anyone. Remember how you're always saying people should be fair?"

"I know, I know," said Katie. "But I can't help it with Taffy."

"But what could she be up to?" Jana asked.

"I don't know," said Katie. "But I just don't trust her."

"Hey, that's some ugly boyfriend you've got," called a ninth-grade boy. He pointed to Rex as Jana squeezed through the crowded hallways after the bell dismissing classes.

"Yeah, I bet he's a terrible kisser," said his friend.

Jana ignored them. Those were the kind of comments she had heard from eighth- and ninth-graders all day long. At the moment she was trying to find Shane, who was supposed to take the two stuffed animals while she went to the yearbook staff room. It would be a relief to get rid of them for a while, thought Jana. It would be hard enough taking care of one baby all day, but when you had two and one of them was almost as big as you were, it was really hard.

Rex and the bunny were a pain, but a lot of other kids were having as much trouble. Tammy Lucero had to fend off boys who wanted to break open her piñata to see if there was any candy in it. Jana had seen Taffy struggling with Monique, her big bear, but at least she only had one animal and had one arm free to carry her books. Clarence Marshall walked around all day with a smile on his face and his mouse sticking out of his shirt pocket. Now and then he would reach up and squeeze it, and everyone would yell, "Child abuse!" or "Mouse abuse!"

Suddenly she spotted Shane. "There you are!"

"Hi, Momma!" he said gleefully. "How are the kids?"

"Fine, but it's your turn to take care of them, remember? Where have you been hiding?"

"I haven't been hiding." He feigned a hurt look. "I've been working hard all day at the office, and now I come home and you don't even have dinner ready."

"Silly," she said, laughing. "Here, take your kids
and the schedule. Don't forget to change them and
give them their formula."

Shane saluted and picked up a baby in each arm.

Jana arrived at the yearbook staff room just as
Funny did. Funny was carrying a green bunny with
red stripes circling it, and it had very long legs with
straps on the bottoms of its feet.

"When I was a little girl, I'd stick my feet in the
straps and dance all around the house with Petey,"
she said, holding the rabbit's feet up for Jana to see.
"Actually, I still do it now and then." She giggled.

They had been working and chatting for a while
when Funny suddenly turned serious. "Jana," she
said, biting her lip. "I shouldn't tell you this, but I'm
going to. Promise you won't tell where you heard
it." Jana had never seen Funny look the way she did.
"It's kind of like snitching on a close friend."

"I promise."

"Laura is really mad at you."

"Mad at ME? What have I done besides stay
alive?"

Funny giggled for a second time and then looked
serious again. "Laura thinks you put Taffy up to
being partners with Randy, and then you asked
Shane to be your partner. She thinks you're out to
get all the good-looking boys for the Mark Twain
girls and are trying to cut us Riverfield girls out."

CHAPTER

10

"*L*aura McCall has no right to be mad at me," Jana said angrily. "She's the one who had that party and was going to ask all the seventh-grade boys, including our boyfriends, and not invite us. *I* should be mad at *her*."

"I know. But she thinks that you're still trying to get even. I really wish you two would try to get along."

Jana sighed and looked at her new friend. She did like Funny so much, and if there was any way in the world she could be close friends with her, she would, but Laura was always making The Fantastic Foursome do nasty things to The Fabulous Five. Such as the time Melissa McConnell ran for class president against Christie. Jana knew that Laura wanted to be sure one of her friends was president. And she certainly wasn't trying to be friends at Bumpers the other day when Jana was talking to Randy.

Jana changed the subject. "How many kids did you call about having their pictures taken?"

Melanie's brown hair was curling in little ringlets around her face, and Beth's still looked damp, when Jana sat down with them in Bumpers. They had had cheerleading practice after school and had barely beaten Jana to the hangout. Beth was holding her panda, but Melanie was childless. Jana guessed that Scott must have the walrus.

"Where's Katie?" Beth asked Christie, who had saved them a booth. Christie had her bunny in the tennis outfit sitting on the table with its back against the end of the booth.

"I saw her after class and she said she had Teen Court, but she wanted us to save a seat for her," said Christie.

"I'll bet that Tony Calcaterra is in trouble again, and she's defending him," said Jana. The four laughed. Since the Teen Court had been started, Tony had been before it three times. The last time had been for painting "T. C. + K. S." on the school wall. Everybody knew it meant Tony Calcaterra plus Katie Shannon, and it had embarrassed the life out of Katie.

"Katie says she really doesn't like Tony," Melanie said.

"You're kidding," said Beth. "No matter what she says, she likes him."

"Do you really think so?" asked Melanie.

"She just doesn't want to admit it because he's so macho, and she's such a feminist," said Jana. "She thinks she'll be considered less liberated if she ever admits she likes him. I'll bet he asks her for a date and she accepts."

"Sure she will," agreed Christie. "She's gaga over him, and I think he's getting into trouble just so that he can go before the Teen Court and have her stick up for him."

Beth put her hands out to stop the conversation. "Speaking of gaga. Look who's making eyes at whom."

They turned to where she was looking. Taffy Sinclair was standing in the checkout line next to Chad Wallace, and she was smiling up at him as he was paying the cashier.

"I wonder what *that's* all about?" asked Christie.

"It looks as if he's buying her a soda," answered Jana.

Taffy looked toward them at that moment and waved. Jana waved back.

"I guess Chad *is* interested in Taffy, if he's buying her a drink," said Christie. "Maybe we've been wrong about her after all."

Taffy put her hand on Chad's arm and said something to him, and they both laughed. Then she headed for The Fabulous Five's booth.

"Hi, Fabulous Five," she said as she beamed down at them. "It is easier to say hello to all of you that way. How are my favorite people?" Beth rolled her eyes toward the ceiling in obvious disgust.

"Fine, Taffy," said Jana. The others murmured their hellos.

"I was just talking to Chad," Taffy continued. "He's such a riot. He keeps me laughing all the time. The doll just bought me this cola. Wasn't that nice?"

Jana thought that Taffy was making an awful big deal about his buying her a soda. But that's Taffy, she thought.

"Isn't the Family Living project a ball?" Taffy asked. "Randy is taking care of our baby right now. He's supposed to be here pretty soon to give it to me."

Jana gritted her teeth to keep from saying anything. She hated to hear Taffy's talking about Randy as if they were married.

Taffy seemed to wait a moment for someone else to speak, and when they didn't, she went on.

"I hear Shane's your partner, Jana, and I saw you at school with a dinosaur. What a big baby. It looked as if you could barely carry it and your books, too."

"It's big, all right," muttered Jana. What was Taffy getting at, anyway? she wondered.

"Oh, Jana. I hate to ask you this, but I just re-membered. I have an appointment with my studio this evening, and I wonder if you could sit for me. It will only be for a couple of hours."

"Gee, Taffy, I don't know. I'm going to have Rex and my bunny, and I've got a lot of homework."

"Oh," said Taffy, looking hurt. "I thought that since I was doing *you* a favor by keeping Laura away from Randy and you were going to be home anyway, you wouldn't mind. I even thought you said . . ." She didn't finish the sentence, but it was clear she thought Jana owed her for what she had done.

Jana flushed. "Shane is supposed to bring Rex and my bunny by, too. I don't think I can get all three of them and my books home."

"Oh, that's all right," Taffy said brightly. "I'll drop Monique off after supper and pick her up after my appointment. Mother won't mind stopping by your apartment. Thanks, Jana," she said before Jana could protest. "You're a *true* friend. See you all later, Fabulous Five." Jana was about to protest further, but with a swish of her skirt Taffy spun on her heel and was gone, leaving Jana with her mouth open.

"Wow, did you get sucked into that," said Beth.

"No, I didn't," Jana protested weakly. "I did say I'd do it the other day, and since I'm not going anywhere anyway, it won't make any difference."

"Well, don't you think it's funny that the favor your biggest enemy is doing for you means she gets to spend time with your boyfriend?" Christie asked suspiciously.

Jana felt helpless to answer. Taffy had said she

wouldn't be Randy's partner if Jana didn't want her to, and hadn't Chad just bought Taffy a soda? And Randy said Taffy talked about being Jana's friend. Wasn't all that proof that Taffy wasn't trying to pull something? It wasn't that she was taking Taffy at her word. Or did she just want it to be that way so badly that she was blinded to what was really going on?

After dinner, Jana sat in her room looking at the animals that surrounded her at her desk. Randy had arrived at Bumpers with Shane and had carried Rex home for her. There had been a brief moment of euphoria when Randy had leaned forward, and this time, instead of her forehead, he had kissed her on the lips. The world had turned to sunshine and roses for her at that very moment. Later Taffy had come by in her mother's car and dropped off the bear.

"Hi, Jana."

Jana hadn't heard her mother come in. "Hi, Mom!"

"My goodness, you've got even more animals. Who does the bear belong to?"

"That's Monique. It's Taffy's. I'm babysitting it for her while she keeps an appointment."

Her mother looked at her curiously. She's probably wondering why I'm doing it, too, thought Jana. Her mother knew that she and Taffy had been enemies all through Mark Twain Elementary.

After she finished her homework, Jana went into the kitchen to make up another batch of formula. All it was was water and cream of wheat, but it looked like real formula, and besides, she was getting rid of a lot of yucky cream of wheat.

Her mother sat at the table. She had papers and receipts pertaining to the wedding spread out in front of her, and she was looking over the guest list. Jana walked to the table and looked over her shoulder. Her father's name wasn't on the list.

"Mom, could I have some invitations? I promised to invite Christie, Beth, Katie, and Melanie, and I've been so busy with school and yearbook that I forgot."

Her mother looked up and smiled. "Sure, sweetheart. I've been meaning to ask you about your friends, but I'm afraid that I forgot, too." She slid several invitations toward Jana from a stack of extras on the table. Jana took the spare ballpoint pen that was lying on the table and addressed the invitations to her friends.

When she finished, she stared at the list for a moment. She hadn't really paid much attention to it before. She read it over and then asked, "Is that the whole list?"

"Ummm, hmm," her mother answered absently. "Except for your friends, of course."

"Aren't you inviting any of our relatives except for Grandmother and Grandfather Drake?"

Her mother shook her head. "None of your aunts, uncles, or cousins live near enough to come. But your grandmother and grandfather will definitely be here. They're driving in on Friday before the wedding and will be staying at a hotel." Jana slid into a depression. Grandma and Grandpa Drake were her mother's parents. Jana loved them, but she had thought her mother might say she was also asking Jana's father.

Back in her room Jana sat at her desk, thinking. She reached into the pocket of her jeans skirt and pulled out an invitation and an envelope. Her mother had extras and wouldn't miss one. Should she send her father an invitation? How mad would her mother be if she did?

Jana pulled open the desk drawer. Inside was the wrinkled letter she had begun the day before. The teardrop had formed an inky circle where it had fallen. She took the letter out and placed it at the corner of her desk.

Next she went to her closet and got an old boot box down from the shelf. Inside was a stack of used envelopes that the support-payment checks used to come in when her father was still sending them. They were all alike, and she had quit collecting them after a while. Underneath the stack were four letters bound together with a rubber band. Jana pulled one free. It was wrinkled and smudged because of the many times she had taken it out to read the letter inside. In the upper left-hand corner of the envelope was written *Bill Morgan*, followed by an address. Carefully she copied the address onto the invitation envelope.

CHAPTER

11

"Where am I going to put all of these?" Pink's voice came from the living room.

"Oh, my word," Jana's mother's voice followed. "I didn't know there were so many. Jana, honey! Can you come and help?"

When Jana reached the living room, she found it filled with boxes, and Pink was standing at the door, sweat glistening from his forehead and perspiration stains darkening his T-shirt. "I'll bring in another load if you ladies want to find a place to put my bowling trophies," he said, grinning. His blond hair was wet and mussed as if he had been in a wrestling match.

"Oh, dear," said Jana's mother. "Where will we put all of these?" She was standing beside two extra-large boxes, set apart from the others, with the words BOWLING TROPHIES written on their sides with black Magic Marker.

"We could rent one of those storage places and move Pink and his trophies into it," volunteered Jana quickly.

Her mother looked sternly at her. "That was *not* a nice remark, young lady."

"I was *only* kidding," Jana insisted, thinking to herself that she would absolutely explode if her mother got any more paranoid between now and the wedding.

Her mother gave her a long look and then followed Pink downstairs. Before she turned away, Jana saw a flash of anger in her eyes.

Laura McCall stood with her feet planted firmly in front of Jana, blocking her way. Under one arm was a stuffed unicorn, and she had the tail of her braid in her other hand, switching it back and forth as if she were a cat who had cornered a mouse. Melissa McConnell and Tammy Lucero stood on either side of her looking angry, and Funny Hawthorne was just behind them, looking thoroughly miserable. Jana faced them by herself, her books and bunny in one arm and Rex clutched in the other. None of her friends were in sight, and she felt vulnerable.

"You're not going to get away with stealing Riverfield boys, Jana Morgan. It was a sneaky trick to get

Taffy to be partners with Randy Kirwan while you lured Shane into being your partner. Who are you going after next?"

"I didn't ask Shane to be partners. He asked me," Jana said angrily, glaring back at Laura. She wasn't stealing Riverfield boys. All she wanted was to keep Randy, who had been her boyfriend in Mark Twain Elementary.

"Do you deny that you asked Taffy to be Randy's partner so he couldn't be mine?"

Jana hadn't, but she couldn't say so without its sounding like a lie. Taffy had brought up the subject of being Randy's partner, not Jana, but Jana had agreed to it. And how did Laura know Jana had agreed to Taffy's asking Randy, anyway?

"I don't need to steal boys from anyone," Jana shot back, avoiding Laura's question. "They go out with whomever they want to. If they don't ask you to be partners, you're the one with a problem."

"*Right!*" said Katie, sticking out her chin. She had appeared from nowhere and stepped between Jana and Laura. Christie and Melanie moved in beside her, too.

"Listen, Katie Shannon," said Melissa. "The only boyfriend you can get is in trouble all the time."

Melissa was referring to Tony Calcaterra, and Jana thought Katie's red hair was going to burst into flame. Then she noticed that Funny looked as if she were going to cry and remembered what she had said about Jana's being the only one able to stop the war between the two cliques. But Laura had started the argument. She had gotten in front of Jana and stopped her. Funny's eyes were pleading with her.

"Well, you can think what you want, Laura Mc-Call," said Jana, backing off. "But I am not out to steal Riverfield boys. And you can shout all you want, but we don't have to listen. Come on, everybody," she ordered Katie, Melanie, Beth, and Christie, "let's find better company." She saw a look of relief on Funny's face as they turned away and left The Fantastic Foursome standing in the hall by themselves.

"The nerve of that witch," said Beth. "If we wanted to, stealing boyfriends from them would be like stealing candy from a baby."

"She's just mad because she couldn't get Randy to be her partner," said Katie. "I guess you were right about Taffy. If it weren't for her, Laura might be Randy's partner right now."

"But what I can't understand," said Jana thoughtfully, "is how Laura *knew* that Taffy asked Randy to be partners so that Laura couldn't ask him."

"Maybe someone overheard you and Taffy talking and told her," said Melanie. "It could have been some Riverfield kid. What about Funny? Did you say anything about your deal with Taffy to her?"

"No. I didn't tell anyone except you guys."

"Maybe Taffy told someone," said Christie.

"Why would she do that?" asked Jana.

The Fabulous Five stared blankly at each other.

"Oh, Jana, there you are. I've been looking all over for you." Taffy seemed out of breath and was hugging her big white stuffed bear with both arms. "I want you to know how much I appreciate your sitting with Randy's and my baby last night. That was *super* of you. If I can do it for you sometime, let me know. That is, if I don't have an appointment."

"You're welcome, Taffy. Your dropping it off and picking it up made it easy."

"Oh, good. Uh, Jana. I was wondering . . . since it was so easy and all . . . if you'd mind sitting again for me? I hate to ask you, but I've got a tryout for this *big* modeling job, and it means a lot to me. Would you mind too much?" Her voice was like syrup being poured over pancakes.

Jana hesitated. It hadn't been so hard sitting the extra make-believe baby. After all, Taffy and her mother had delivered it to her apartment and picked it up later. All Jana had to do was carry it to her room and let it sit with Rex. The Tyrannosaurus rex dinosaur and the bear wearing a tutu made an interesting couple.

"I guess so, Taffy."

"Oh, thank you *so* much, Jana. I'll drop it off again, just as I did before."

"Great," answered Jana. "When do you want me to sit?"

"Saturday."

"Saturday? Taffy, I *can't* sit Saturday. I've got to go shopping for a dress for Mom's wedding Saturday morning."

"That's okay, Jana. My appointment is in the afternoon. I'll drop it off around one o'clock."

"But I'm going to the football game with Trumbull! Besides, don't you have to cheer?"

"Jana . . . you aren't going back on your promise, are you?" Taffy sounded as if her feelings were badly hurt. Then she said softly, "Miss Wolfe understands. She gave me permission to miss the game because my appointment is so important. I was counting on you to understand, too. After my trying so hard to help you keep Randy out of Laura McCall's clutches. And I thought we were starting to be friends. . . ."

Jana felt guilty. Taffy *had* helped her, but the football game was important to Jana, and she was supposed to see Randy after the game. How could she go to the game with all the stuffed animals— especially Rex and Monique? They were so big. She wouldn't be able to get through the crowd, let alone find seats for herself, the dinosaur, and the bear.

But Taffy had helped her, Jana thought. She *was* acting like Jana's friend and Jana owed her. She looked at Taffy standing in front of her. How could she be so uncaring after Taffy had been so much help?

Jana sighed. "I'll do it, Taffy."

CHAPTER

12

"If you put the dinosaur in that chair and put the rabbit in its lap, I think they'll be all right," the sales clerk said. Jana could see the Mayfair Dress Shop clerk was suppressing a smile.

Jana's mother had been as excited as if she were the one who was going to get the new dress when they started out that morning with Pink driving them to the mall. Jana sat in the backseat of the car with Rex and the bunny. She must have tried on a zillion dresses since then, but it was the same in all the shops, and Mayfair was their last hope. Her mother's smile had faded a long time ago.

Jana held an armload of dresses as her mother rifled through a dress rack trying to find others for Jana to try on. Pink sat in the chair next to Rex and the pink bunny and smiled at everything that was going on around him.

"That's just about all I can find," said her mother. "Why don't you try these on, Jana, and for goodness' sake, I hope there's one you like. The wedding is in one week."

The sales clerk gave Jana four dressing-room tags, which Jana knew was one more than was usually allowed. The clerk seemed to be sympathetic to their endless search.

Jana hung the dresses on the wall hook in the dressing room, putting the lavender one at the back. She tried on the first one and took it off immediately. It was blue with a tight little collar and it made her look as if she were ninety years old. The next one was white and green polka dots with a big bow at the neck. It was strange and didn't warrant a trip to show her mother either.

The third one was the one Jana had liked. It was navy blue and had a tight skirt with a vent in back that Jana thought looked sophisticated. The sleeves were kind of short beneath shoulder pads and the dress made her look a lot older, like a high school senior.

When she marched out to the showroom to model for her mother, the look in her mother's eyes told her she didn't feel the same way. Jana stood between the three mirrors and swung around looking at herself from all sides. "I like it," she said with a hint of defiance in her voice.

Her mother waited a moment before speaking. "Jana, don't you think it's a little too old for you?"

Jana gritted her teeth and tried to keep a tight little smile on her face. "But I *like* it." She could feel tears pushing their way into her eyes. There's nothing to cry about, she told herself. It was just a dumb dress.

"Jana, why don't you try on the lavender one with the puffy sleeves. It's so pretty."

Jana knew the lavender one had been her mother's favorite. "Why can't I have this one?"

Her mother took a deep breath. "Jana . . ."

"I'll take the lavender one. *It's your wedding.*" Jana wished she hadn't said it when she saw her mother's face. She looked as if she were going to cry. Pink sat in his chair next to Rex and the pink rabbit, looking equally miserable. It's the two of them against me, Jana thought. She turned quickly and went back to the dressing room so they wouldn't see the tears running down her cheeks.

Later, Jana lay on her bed with a pillow scrunched in her arms that was damp from her tears. The lavender dress hung on her closet door. It had been a perfect fit. Across the room Rex sat next to her desk chair where Taffy's bear was sitting. The pink bunny, with no name, was on the bed with her.

The ride home from the mall had been made in silence. She could see her mother's back was ramrod straight. Jana had gone directly to her room and had only come out when Taffy brought the bear.

Jana was miserable. On top of that she knew she

was making her mother miserable, too. She didn't want to do that, but she didn't seem to be able to stop it, either. Things were piling onto her too fast.

The clock on her bureau ticked away. It was going on three P.M., and everyone but her was at the football game. Everyone but Taffy and me she corrected herself, remembering that Taffy had said she had a modeling appointment.

Jana sat up and wiped her eyes with the back of her hand. The pink bunny her father had given her fell against her leg, and she picked it up. It was beginning to look old, she thought. She had had it for almost ten years. That was even before the last time she had seen her father. She guessed she would probably *never* see him after her mother and Pink got married.

Jana climbed out of bed and went to her desk and opened the top drawer. The letter to her father and the invitation lay on top, and she took them out and returned to the bed. She opened the letter and reread it. It didn't seem like a very good letter now. What would her father think when he read it? Would he think she was a child? Would he think she was begging him to come and see her? *Well, she wasn't.* He had to want to see her, too. It couldn't be just one way.

The last of the four letters she had from him had been written two years ago when he wrote about the vacation out west. He had not even bothered to come for her. Some father he was. Pink would *definitely* make a better father.

She sighed, remembering how her mother had always been there for her. Whenever she had problems, her mother was always there to help. Jana looked at the lavender dress hanging on the door. She dropped the letter and the invitation next to bunny, then went over to take the dress down.

When she stepped into the living room, her mother and Pink were sitting together quietly. Pink noticed her first, and his face brightened. He reached over and touched her mother on the knee.

Jana walked into the center of the room and pirouetted in front of them. The skirt of the lavender dress billowed out as if it were a prom dress. Before coming out of her room, she had brushed her hair and put on some lip gloss and now she smiled as brightly as she could. She saw her mother's eyes brimming with tears. "How do I look?"

"Gorgeous, honey. Just gorgeous," said her mother.

Pink was smiling as if he had just won a first-place bowling trophy. The three of them sat in the living room and talked about the wedding for a while before Jana went to her room to change back into her jeans.

She was still lonely, but she felt better. Everything was going to be okay. Her mother deserved to marry Pink, and it wasn't right for Jana to fight their being together. She had known that all along, but she had been so used to having her mother to herself that she couldn't stand sharing her.

Jana tuned her radio to the local station, hoping she could hear the score of the Wakeman-Trumbull foot-ball game, but all she could get was world news and music. She had wondered about how the game was going all afternoon. Now it's halftime, she thought. I wonder if Randy has thrown a touchdown pass or made a big run? Now it's at least the fourth quarter; is Wakeman ahead or behind? She couldn't stand being all alone, so she got two Wacko Junior High pennants and put them in Rex's and Monique's paws as if they were rooting for Wacko, too. She put a pom-pom in the pink bunny's lap.

When she knew the game was over, Jana thought about calling Bumpers to talk to her friends, but she would only be more lonely and depressed. Darn that Taffy. Why did she have to have an appointment on Saturday afternoon, anyway? Next time Jana would have to tell her to get another sitter. Her feeling of being obligated to Taffy could only go so far.

"What kind of pizza do you want?" asked Pink. It was his usual question on the nights that he and her mother were going bowling.

"Deep-dish, pepperoni, green pepper, and mush-room." It was the answer she always gave him.

"Want me to order a large this time? You're grow-ing up, and it takes more to fill you up," he said, smiling.

"No, regular is fine." She smiled back, trying to show him she appreciated the offer. Pink was a good guy. At least he tried, which is more than she could say for her father. She noticed how natural he and her mother looked together when they walked out the door.

When the pizza came, Jana turned on the televi-sion and got a soda before opening the box and set-ting it on a trophy box next to the couch. She looked at her watch. She would eat first and then call Beth to see if she was home yet and find out how the game had gone.

As she was tearing out the second slice of pizza, the phone rang. It was Christie, and Jana could hear Beth, Katie, and Melanie in the background.

"Jana! You'll never guess what!" cried Christie.

Jana expected Beth or Melanie to sound so melo-dramatic, but never Christie. "Calm down, Christie. Did Randy get hurt? Is he all right? Slow down and tell me."

"It's worse, Jana. Much worse." Christie paused for a breath. "We went to the game and Randy didn't get hurt, but guess who was there."

"Who?"

"Taffy. She was there from start to finish, and after the game was over she latched onto Randy at Bumpers, and she talked him into taking her to a movie."

Jana sat stunned. The pizza slice bent in her hand and a mushroom fell on the floor.

CHAPTER

13

"*B*ut she couldn't have been at the game," Jana insisted. "She had a modeling appointment. She said it was important to her. I've been sitting here all afternoon with her bear and Rex because of it."

"I know. We were there when she asked you to sit. But she was definitely at the game, cheering like crazy. I think that you've been *had*," said Christie.

"But what about her asking me if it was okay to be Randy's partner? And she said she was crazy about Chad Wallace. We saw Chad buy her a soda, didn't we?"

"I don't think so."

"You don't think so, what?"

"I don't think we saw Chad buy her a soda. Melanie was talking to Garrett Boldt about Taffy's liking Chad, and Garrett said Chad told him that Taffy gave him money and asked him to pay for her soda. Also, he said he thought Taffy was hanging around outside school in the morning waiting for him. Then she's been walking onto the school ground with him as if they were together. He thinks she's kind of spacey."

"Why, that rat!" exclaimed Jana. "I'll bet she told Randy she wanted to be friends with me just so he'd tell me she said it. She's been faking being friends and acting as if she were interested in Chad just so I'd say it was okay for her to ask Randy to be partners on the Family Living project."

"That's what we think, too."

"And she must have asked me to sit Monique so she could go to the football game. She knew I wouldn't be able to go because I couldn't carry her darn bear, my pink bunny, and Rex, too."

The more Jana talked, the madder she got. By the time she hung up the phone she was ready to kill Taffy Sinclair. She was stomping back and forth in the living room, shouting at an imaginary Taffy. By the time the doorbell rang a few minutes later, Jana was ready to blast her.

"TAFFY SINCLAIR, I'M GOING TO . . ." Jana's voice faltered as she saw Mr. Sinclair standing on the porch by himself.

"Taffy's not with me," he said in his soft voice. "She called and asked me if I'd come by and pick up her bear. She said to tell you you're a true friend."

Jana looked at him in disbelief. Taffy had the nerve to continue the farce. She expected Jana to go on believing her lies.

Thinking quickly, she said, "It's not legal for students' parents to sit with our make-believe babies, Mr. Sinclair. I wouldn't want Taffy to get a bad grade if someone found out. Why don't I keep Monique? I'll return it tomorrow if my mother's fiancé will give me a ride."

"Oh, uh . . . I guess that's okay. I'll tell her. I'm sure she'll be grateful."

"Good-bye, Mr. Sinclair," Jana said with a smile.

When he had left, Jana picked up the phone and dialed Funny's number. She just might be home by now.

"Hello," Funny answered the phone.

"Hi. It's Jana."

"Oh, hi. I missed you at the game. It was great. We won and Randy scored two touchdowns. Where were you, anyway?"

"It's a long, terrible story, and I'll tell you about it. But first I need to know something. Who told Laura that I asked Taffy to be partners with Randy so Laura couldn't be?"

"Taffy did. That's why Laura was so mad. Taffy said you didn't want Laura even to think about being Randy's partner on the Family Living project. You're not going to try and get back at Laura are you, Jana? She just thought you were being mean."

"No, I'm not. For once it's not Laura's fault. Taffy

told me that Laura was trying to get Randy to be her partner and that if I wanted, she would ask him so that Laura couldn't. She did all kinds of things to make me believe her."

"Oh, that's terrible. I heard you and Taffy had clubs against each other in Mark Twain Elementary, but you seemed to be getting along okay now."

"I might just start up my club again. Thanks for the terrific idea, Funny. Oh, Funny . . . tell Laura that I did not ask Shane to be partners. He did truly ask me. I'm not trying to steal Riverfield boys."

"Thanks, Jana." There was a smile in Funny's voice again. "I'm glad to hear that. I'll tell her."

Jana hung up the phone and went to her room to make plans. Boy, was she going to make Taffy pay for her nasty tricks.

CHAPTER

14

The next morning Jana slept late. When she woke, she was surrounded by the happy faces of all the animals stacked around her room. She was getting used to the silly look on Rex's face, and even Monique seemed to be smiling.

Her mother had the papers spread out and was drinking coffee in the living room. Jana dug out the funnies, sat on the opposite end of the couch, and pulled her robe up around her. Sunday mornings were always the best. Jana loved the quiet time when her mother sipped her coffee and seemed much more relaxed than she was during the week, when she was working.

Jana had worked her way to the middle of the cartoon section and had started to read *Peanuts* when her mother broke the silence. "Jana, you do like the lavender dress, don't you?"

"Yes, Mom. I really do." She paused a moment before continuing. "I'm sorry I was such a pain about the dress. I did have things to do, but they weren't as important as the wedding."

Her mother smiled and moved down the couch to put her arms around Jana. "I know, honey. Sometimes it's tough when things are changing so fast. But I want you to know that you'll always be my girl. Pink's and my getting married isn't going to change any of that. You know, I should have been listening to you a little better, too. I realized that you were maybe the more mature of the two of us when you came out wearing the dress yesterday. You kind of told me that I was pretty important to you. I love you for it."

Jana snuggled deep into her mother's arms. "Mom?"

"Yes, sweetheart."

"Pink can keep some of his trophies in my room if he wants."

Her mother pulled back so that she could see Jana better. She smiled sweetly and tears filled her eyes. "Thank you, Jana. Do you know what Pink suggested last night at the bowling alley?"

"No, I am *not* learning how to bowl," said Jana, laughing. "Christie's dad wants her to play tennis with him all the time, and she doesn't want to. It's okay if you two go bowling without me."

"That's not what he suggested at all. What he said, young lady, was that we ought to raise your allowance."

"Raise my allowance?"

"Yes. With two of us working we can do that now. I wasn't able to do it before."

"I know. Your job didn't pay enough."

"One other thing. Now that Pink is going to be around, I won't be such a worrywart about you. It's hard when you're the only parent, you have to think of everything, and you get overly protective because you're afraid something might happen that you can't handle. So you're probably going to see a little relaxing of the rules around here. But don't try to get away with anything. There will also be two of us to mete out the punishment," she said with a gleam in her eyes.

Later, in her room, Jana took the letter and the invitation from the desk drawer. She went to the closet and pulled out the boot box and put them in with her father's letters and the support-payment envelopes. Maybe I'll see him again someday, she thought as she put the box back. The wedding was her mother's and Pink's, and her father didn't really belong there.

She picked up the pink bunny and stroked it. Things were changing a lot, as her mother had said. They were even changing between the members of The Fabulous Five. Everyone was getting so many things to do, but she knew when she called them later, after she had talked to Taffy, they would all jump in to help her with her plan. She straightened the rabbit's ears. Maybe it was time to give him a name. Since he was pink, she would call him Little Pink, and Pink would probably be thrilled.

"Oh, hi, Jana." Taffy's voice sounded cheerful over the phone.

"Hi, Taffy. I guess your dad told you what I said."

"Yes, and thanks. You were right. If anyone found out that my parents sat with Monique, I'd get my grade knocked down. You *are* a good friend."

"How was your appointment?"

Taffy sounded cautious when she answered, "Oh . . . it was okay. A typical modeling job, hot lights and all."

"Since we're friends now, I'd like to see you model sometime."

"I think that would be all right."

"Taffy, I called to tell you I won't be able to bring the bear by today. Pink's not here. But instead of you and your dad picking it up, why don't I just bring it to school in the morning?"

"That would be super, but won't that be a lot of trouble?"

To Jana's delight, Taffy sounded relieved, as if she thought the two of them were still friends.

"Oh, don't worry, Taffy, it's not too much trouble," Jana assured her.

After hanging up with Taffy, Jana quickly dialed Christie, Melanie, Beth, and Katie. Later, when each of them had arrived, she grabbed sodas and settled everyone in her room. And then she said in her most solemn voice, "I hereby call this meeting of The Against Taffy Sinclair Club to order."

CHAPTER

15

"*T*here she is." Katie pointed at Taffy, who was walking onto the school ground with Chad Wallace on Monday morning. Taffy was chattering away as if Chad and she were old friends. He was looking around and not paying the slightest bit of attention to her.

"When you know the truth, it's pretty obvious, isn't it?" muttered Jana.

"It sure is," answered Christie. "He's totally ignoring her."

Christie had her bunny. Melanie was holding her walrus. Beth had her panda, and Katie, her Sheena doll. Jana had Rex and Little Pink. Taffy saw them and headed for them with a smile on her face.

When she reached them, she looked puzzled. "Where's Monique?" she asked.

"I've got some bad news, Taffy." Jana tried to look serious, but it was all she could do to stifle a giggle. "Monique's been bear-napped."

"She's been what?" Taffy looked horrified.

"Bear-napped. I brought her to school this morning and set her and Rex down outside the girls' room while I went in, and when I came out, she was gone."

"What do you mean, *gone*? How could she be gone? Who would have taken her?"

"She's just gone, as in a missing-person, or I should say, a missing-bear."

"*Jana Morgan, what are you trying to pull?*"

"Pull? Why nothing, Taffy," said Jana in her sweetest voice. "Friends don't pull things on each other, do they?" Taffy gave her a suspicious look as she added, "Where did you say your appointment was on Saturday? The Cinema-six?"

Taffy's face fell.

"Seen any good movies lately, Taffy?" Katie asked.

Taffy turned from one member of The Fabulous Five to the next with a look of horror on her face. Then the horror turned to anger, and she whipped around and glared at Jana.

"Jana Morgan, if you don't give Monique back right away, I'll tell Randy. It's his project, too, you know. If I fail because the bear's lost, he fails, also."

"Gee, Taffy. What are you going to tell Randy? That you tricked me into taking care of your bear so you could steal him from me? How about your telling Laura that it was my idea for you to ask Randy to be partners with you? Funny Hawthorne will vouch for that. I don't think Randy would like to hear any of that, do you?"

Taffy's face turned bright red and her lips tightened. She was trapped—and she knew it.

"Monique's got to be around somewhere," Jana said. "We'll help you look for her, won't we, gang?" They all nodded enthusiastically. "If we find her, we'll let you know."

Taffy spun on her heel and stormed away.

"Boy, is she mad," said Beth.

Jana smiled gleefully at the way things were going so far. "It serves her right. You know, I think she must have gotten the idea about asking me to bear-sit when she saw that Shane and I were using Rex as a make-believe baby. She knew I wouldn't be able to take him and Monique anywhere together. They're just too big to cart around."

"I agree," said Christie. "The first time she asked was probably a setup to see if she could talk you into it."

"Now," said Jana, "we've got to put the rest of the plan into effect. It wouldn't make me feel too bad if Taffy got in trouble because she had lost the bear, but I don't want Randy to get into trouble."

She raised her hand, and The Fabulous Five did a

group high-five. "Let's go team!" they shouted in unison.

Taffy came into the cafeteria at lunchtime and glared angrily at The Fabulous Five before sitting down with Stacy Holgrem and Gloria Drexler.

"She's really upset," said Melanie. "Her Family Living class is tomorrow, and she's got to find the bear before that or Mrs. Blankenship will know something is wrong. Oh, look. Randy's going over to talk to her."

"Oh, boy, I'd sure like to know what he's saying," said Katie. "He's probably asking her where Monique is."

"Talk to him, Jana," urged Christie. "See what you can find out."

As Randy left Taffy's table, Jana waved to him, and he came over.

"Hi, I heard you had a great game on Saturday. I wish I could have been there."

He smiled. "I looked for you. What happened? Did you get held up buying stuff for your mom's wedding?"

"No," she said quickly. "I had a big babysitting job. I hear you went to a movie later."

Randy looked embarrassed. "Taffy and I did. She said she wanted to see *The Return of the Vampire* real badly, and she was afraid to go with just girls. She talked me into going. It was kind of dumb. It wasn't a date, though," he added.

"Did you have to buy a ticket for Monique?" Jana asked, smiling up at him.

"No. Taffy said she had a cousin who was visiting, and she left the bear with her. That way she wouldn't break the rule about having parents sit."

"A cousin, huh? Where's the bear now?" Jana asked innocently.

"That's what I was just asking Taffy." He frowned. "I guess her cousin still has it. Mrs. Blankenship isn't going to like it when she looks at our report and finds out that someone besides Taffy or me was taking care of it all weekend and today, too. I told Taffy to get it back right away, and I'd take it. She acted kind of funny."

"I'm sure she'll get it back," said Jana.

"I am, too, but if she doesn't do it quickly it could lower our grades. I've gotta go. If you're going to be at Bumpers later I'll walk you home."

"Great," said Jana.

"Okay, everybody," she said after Randy left. "It's time for part B of our plan. Melanie, do you have the note?"

They caught up with Taffy as she left the cafeteria. "Oh, Taffy. We may be able to help you find Monique," Jana said with a big smile.

"You'd *better* help me find Monique," Taffy said nastily.

"I found this note from the bearnapper on my desk in history class. I thought you might want it."

Taffy grabbed the paper from her hand and read it hurriedly out loud:

"If the owner of the white bear wearing a tutu wants it returned, she should go to the girls' room by the main entrance and look behind the water tank in the first stall."

Taffy looked at Jana. "This is some kind of trick, isn't it?"

Jana shrugged. "How should we know? We're just delivering the note."

"Jana Morgan, I'll get you for this if it's the last thing I ever do!" As Taffy left in a huff, The Fabulous Five doubled over and put their hands over their mouths, so that Taffy wouldn't hear the peals of laughter that were ringing out behind her.

"Did everyone put their notes where they're supposed to be?" asked Jana when they had all recovered. Her friends nodded, and for the first time in weeks Jana felt great. She was their leader again, and they were all working together to get even with their old enemy. Things hadn't really changed much after all.

The Fabulous Five got to Bumpers early and found a booth near the old Wurlitzer jukebox. Soon afterward Randy, Keith, and Scott came in. Randy saw Monique sitting on top of the jukebox and walked over to it. He looked angry as he took it down and carried it to a booth where he sat it on the table.

The girls put their hands over their mouths to suppress their giggles. Randy was frowning and talking to his friends loudly. Then the door burst open and Taffy came flying in. She was perspiring and her hair was messed up. It was obvious that she had been running all over the place. She glanced around the room frantically, and then a look of horror came over her face when she saw the bear on the table and Randy looking at her. He was obviously not pleased.

Randy got up and carried the bear over to Taffy. Jana and her friends strained to hear what he was saying, but the sound of the jukebox drowned out their conversation. Jana could tell he was chewing Taffy out for leaving the bear on the machine and jeopardizing their Family Living grade. But what could Taffy say? She couldn't tell him that Jana had put the bear there to get back at Taffy for her dirty tricks.

Jana smiled broadly. The note behind the water tank in the girls' room had only been the beginning. It had started Taffy on a wild-goose chase that took her from place to place where other notes, which The Fabulous Five had made up at Jana's apartment on Sunday, sent her on to the next location. The last note had said that if Taffy hurried, she would find the bear at Bumpers.

Jana had a feeling that Randy wouldn't be in a very good mood when he walked her home from Bumpers. But she was sure, since she was feeling so good herself, that she could cheer him up.

CHAPTER

16

*O*rgan music swelled from the pipes and filled the church with beautiful sounds. Jana looked down the long aisle to the back of the church where her mother was coming through the door with Grandpa Drake. She wore a sea-green silk chiffon dress and was holding the most beautiful bouquet of flowers Jana had ever seen. She looks like a goddess, thought Jana.

Her mother walked with her arm through Grandpa Drake's as they paced slowly, in time to the music, toward the altar where Jana was standing. Jana looked across at Pink, who was dressed in a black tuxedo, his face beaming with a glow that was almost angelic. Jana had wondered if he would show up at the church in a fancy bowling shirt, but she had been afraid to ask her mother about it.

When they reached the altar, Pink stepped forward and took her mother's arm, and Grandpa Drake went to sit with Grandma Drake in the first row. Jana smiled at them and then looked to the row behind them. It was filled with Melanie, who was crying softly, Christie, Beth, and Katie. In between them sat a walrus, a bunny in a tennis outfit, a panda bear, and a Sheena doll. On the end, next to the aisle, sat Rex with Little Pink on his lap. Behind them sat Randy, looking as handsome as he could possibly be and smiling his 1,000-watt smile at her. Jana smiled back, feeling instantly shy.

The minister started to speak and Jana turned. She listened to his words and tried to imagine what Randy and she would look like standing in front of him. She would have on the most beautiful wedding gown in the world. It would sweep to the floor and would be made of milky-white lace covered with glittering sequins. A long veil would partially hide her face, and she would be carrying a huge bouquet of flowers. They would both say, "I do," and Randy would lift her veil, look into her eyes, and kiss her ever so tenderly. Tears were running down her cheeks.

"Jana, it's time for you to get out of the bathroom and give one of us a chance," her mother said through the door. "Pink and I have to get ready, too, you know."

Jana sighed as she untangled her curling-iron cord from the cord of Pink's electric razor. She had been having a hard time finding her things now that his dryer, hairbrush, razor, toothbrush, and other stuff added to the clutter on top of an already cluttered counter. Jana did appreciate the five-dollar increase in her allowance, and she did appreciate being able to stay out a half hour later on Fridays and Saturdays, but she didn't appreciate the pressure of having to hurry out of the bathroom.

Other than having to squeeze Pink's things in, everything had gone pretty well since the wedding. Pink had set his favorite trophies on top of the television and stored the rest of them in their space in the basement of the apartment building.

Jana hummed to herself as she brushed her hair. The Family Living project had ended two days before, and it was going to be nice not to have to carry that darn dinosaur around, especially since Randy had asked her to go to a movie on Friday and she could stay out later now. She thought maybe he was feeling a little guilty about going to the movie with Taffy, even though he had said it wasn't a real date.

She and her friends had all gotten good grades on the project, and Shane said he was glad to take Rex back because Igor hadn't been sleeping well without him. Randy and Taffy had gotten good grades, too, but Taffy still wasn't speaking to Jana. It was just like the good old days at Mark Twain Elementary when they didn't speak most of the time.

Jana turned off the water and dried her hands. "Okay, I'm finished," she said as she opened the door. "Mom, can't we get another bathroom? With three of us there's never enough time."

"There would be if one of us wouldn't spend so much time on her hair, young lady."

"Well, you taught me to be neat," she said with a smirk.

Her mother wrinkled her nose at Jana in response and went into the bathroom.

Jana's mind was on the beautiful wedding and the reception afterward as she dressed, and she was hanging up her robe in the closet when she noticed the boot box on the shelf. She would have to tell her father about the wedding when she sent him his Christmas card. Then she hummed to herself as she made her bed and turned to leave for school. She was almost out of her room when she stopped and went back to the bed. Picking up Little Pink, she gave him a hug and sat him in the position of honor next to Honeybear.

CHAPTER

17

*W*hen the bell rang dismissing school for the day, Melanie rushed through the halls to find her friends. Cheerleading practice had been canceled, and she was dying to go to Bumpers with the rest of The Fabulous Five, sink into a booth, and do absolutely nothing but sip on a soft drink and talk to her friends.

"I had three tests today," she muttered under her breath, "and I deserve a break." Rounding a corner, she almost smacked into Jana and Funny coming toward her deep in conversation.

"Hi, guys," Melanie said brightly. "Anybody for Bumpers?"

"Hi, Mel," Jana and Funny said in unison. They both returned Melanie's smile, and then Jana's face clouded. "I really wish we could, but you wouldn't believe the number of seventh-graders who *still* haven't had their yearbook pictures made. Funny and I have a whole list of names to call this afternoon. Mr. Neal is screaming for those pictures."

"Have a tall, cold one for us," Funny said, licking her lips appreciatively.

"Sure. I understand," Melanie said. "See you guys later."

When she reached her locker, she put away the books from her afternoon classes and pulled out the ones she needed for homework. Christie's locker was next to hers, and just as she slammed her own shut, Christie came bouncing up and began working her combination lock.

"Hi, Melanie," she said breathlessly as she pulled the locker door open. "Oh, rats!" she muttered, frowning. "I forgot to bring my racket and I promised Jon a fast game of tennis before homework. Oh, well," she added with a shrug. "Guess I'll just have to run home and get it. See you later."

Melanie sighed and watched Christie race through the hall, ducking around kids in her hurry to get to the exit. That makes it two down and two to go, she thought as she looked around for Katie or Beth. Surely *they* would want to go to Bumpers with her.

All around her, girls were meeting their friends or walking down the hall together. Alexis and Kim were giggling beside Kim's locker. Gloria Drexler and Marcie Bee were talking to Stacy Holgrem.

"Hey, Melanie. Am I glad I found you."

Melanie whirled around, startled, but pleased to see Beth rushing toward her. "Hi," chirped Melanie. "I was looking for you, too."

"I hate to ask this," Beth began, "but would you do me a huge favor?"

Melanie blinked. "Sure," she said softly. She had a sinking feeling that the favor had nothing to do with Bumpers.

"You walk right past the public library on your way home, right? Well, Drama Club meets today, and I really want to go. Could you turn in this book for me? It's due today." She thrust a large book into Melanie's hand. On the cover was the title *The Plight of the American Indian*. "I could drop it off myself later," Beth continued, "but then I'd be late for dinner. And with four brothers and sisters, being late for dinner means only one thing. *Starvation!*"

Melanie nodded and slid the library book on top of her own books. "Have you seen Katie?" she asked, forcing a smile. "I was hoping she'd want to go to Bumpers with me for a little while."

"I saw her a moment ago," said Beth. "She can't go to Bumpers, though. She's got something else going on. Something to do with Teen Court, I think." Beth shook her head as if she were struggling to remember. "I'm not sure what, but anyway, she's busy."

Melanie leaned against her locker as Beth bounded off to go to her Drama Club meeting. The halls were emptying quickly now, and Melanie felt a lump growing in her throat as she realized that in another few moments she would be standing there totally alone.

"Busy," she muttered. "Katie's busy. Jana's busy. Christie's busy. And now even Beth is busy. Everyone's too busy for *me*."

She sighed deeply and started slowly for home. It's not just today, she thought. It's been happening a lot lately. It's as if none of my friends has time for me anymore.

Melanie was swept by a sudden wave of panic. It *had* been happening a lot lately. Were they mad at her? Had she done something awful that she wasn't even aware of? Something that made them want to avoid her? Or was it more than that? Was The Fabulous Five breaking up?

Find out in *The Fabulous Five #7: The Kissing Disaster*, coming next month.

ABOUT THE AUTHOR

Betsy Haynes, the daughter of a former newswoman, began scribbling poetry and short stories as soon as she learned to write. A serious writing career, however, had to wait until after her marriage and the arrival of her two children. But that early practice must have paid off, for within three months Mrs. Haynes had sold her first story. In addition to a number of magazine short stories and the Taffy Sinclair series, Mrs. Haynes is also the author of *The Great Mom Swap* and its sequel, *The Great Boyfriend Trap*. She lives in Colleyville, Texas, with her husband, who is also an author.

Great FREE offer
just for you!

Join SNEAK PEEKS™!

Do you want to know what's new before anyone else? Do you like to read great books about girls just like you? If you do, then you won't want to miss SNEAK PEEKS™! Be the first of your friends to know what's hot ... When you join SNEAK PEEKS™, we'll send you FREE inside information in the mail about the latest books ... *before they're published!* Plus updates on your favorite series, authors, and exciting new stories filled with friendship and fun ... adventure and mystery ... girlfriends and boyfriends.

It's easy to be a member of SNEAK PEEKS™. Just fill out the coupon below ... and get ready for fun! It's FREE! Don't delay—sign up today!

Mail to: SNEAK PEEKS™,
Bantam Books, P.O. Box 1011,
South Holland, IL 60473

☐ YES! I want to be a member of Bantam's SNEAK PEEKS™ and receive hot-off-the-press information in the mail.

Name _____ Birthdate _____

Address _____

City/State _____ Zip _____

SK31—12/88

Saddle up for great reading with

T·H·E
SADDLE CLUB

A blue-ribbon series by Bonnie Bryant

Stevie, Carole and Lisa are all very different, but they *love* horses! The three girls are best friends at Pine Hollow Stables, where they ride and care for all kinds of horses. Come to Pine Hollow and get ready for all the fun and adventure that comes with being 13!

Don't miss this terrific ten-book series. Collect them all!

☐	**15594-6 HORSE CRAZY #1**	**$2.75**
☐	**15611-X HORSE SHY #2**	**$2.75**
☐	**15626-8 HORSE SENSE #3**	**$2.75**

Watch for other SADDLE CLUB books all year. More great reading—and riding—to come!

Buy them at your local bookstore or use this handy page for ordering.

- -

Bantam Books, Dept. SK34, 414 East Golf Road, Des Plaines, IL 60016

Please send me the books I have checked above. I am enclosing $_____ (please add $2.00 to cover postage and handling). Send check or money order—no cash or C.O.D.s please.

Mr/Ms _____

Address _____

City/State _____ Zip_____

SK34—2/89

Please allow four to six weeks for delivery. This offer expires 8/89.
Prices and availability subject to change without notice.

GOOD NEWS! The five best friends who formed the AGAINST TAFFY SINCLAIR CLUB will be starring in a series all their own.

IT'S NEW. IT'S FUN. IT'S FABULOUS. IT'S THE FABULOUS FIVE!

From Betsy Haynes, the bestselling author of the Taffy Sinclair books, *The Great Mom Swap,* and *The Great Boyfriend Trap,* comes THE FABULOUS FIVE. Follow the adventures of Jana Morgan and the rest of THE FABULOUS FIVE as they begin the new school year in Wakeman Jr. High.

☐ **SEVENTH-GRADE RUMORS (Book #1)** 15625-X $2.75

☐ **THE TROUBLE WITH FLIRTING (Book #2)** 15633-0 $2.75

☐ **THE POPULARITY TRAP (Book #3)** 15634-9 $2.75

☐ **HER HONOR, KATIE SHANNON (Book #4)** 15640-3 $2.75

☐ **THE BRAGGING WAR (Book #5)** 15651-9 $2.75

Watch for a brand new book each and every month!

Book #6 On Sale: February

Buy them at your local bookstore or use this page to order:

Bantam Books, Dept. SK28, 414 East Golf Road, Des Plaines, IL 60016

Please send me the books I have checked above. I am enclosing $_____ (please add $2.00 to cover postage and handling). Send check or money order—no cash or C.O.D.s please.

Mr/Ms _____

Address _____

City/State _____ Zip _____

SK28—2/89

Please allow four to six weeks for delivery. This offer expires 8/89.